The Reaction

Even the book morphs!
Flip the pages
and check it out!

Look for other [ANIMORPHS]™
titles by K.A. Applegate:

ANIMORPHS™

The Reaction

K.A. Applegate

AN
APPLE
PAPERBACK

SCHOLASTIC INC.
New York Toronto London Auckland Sydney

Cover illustration by Damon C. Torres/The I-Way Company

ISBN 0-590-99734-3

10 9 8 7 6 5 4 3 2   7 8 9/9 0 1 2/0

Printed in the U.S.A.   40

First Scholastic printing, November 1997

For Michael

The Reaction

CHAPTER 1

My name is Rachel.

I won't tell you my last name or where I'm from. Here's what I *can* tell you about myself: I'm tall for my age. Maybe tall for *any* age. I have blond hair. I like gymnastics, shopping, and a good fight with bad guys. Not necessarily in that order.

People say I'm pretty, and I guess I'm okay. People say I'm self-confident, and I know that's true.

My closest friends think I'm fearless. They're wrong about that. People without fear are just insane. I have plenty of fear in my life. Some days I feel afraid from the minute I wake up in the morning till my last nightmare at night.

1

But the thing about fear is you can't be afraid of it. I know that sounds confusing. I guess what I mean is, be afraid if you have to, right? Fear is like this vicious little worm that lives inside you and eats you alive. You have to fight it. You have to know it's there. You have to accept that you'll never get rid of it, but fight it just the same.

Brave isn't about not being afraid. It's about being scared to death and still not giving in.

That's all any of us do. Any of us Animorphs. We just try not to give in.

And in the middle of it all, in the middle of all the danger and betrayal and fear, we try to hold on to what's normal and good. Have to keep up with the homework. Have to be ready for that pop quiz. Have to still listen to music and watch TV and maybe go to a movie.

You know what I mean? When you live in an insane world, you have to hold on to the little things.

There are six of us. Five humans, one not-so-human. There's me; there's Jake, my more responsible cousin; Marco, my personal pain in the butt; Cassie, my best friend forever; Tobias, who was our first casualty, trapped forever in the body of a hawk; and Ax, the only Andalite to survive their mission to Earth.

It all began with an innocent walk through an

abandoned construction site at night. The five of us, minus Ax, were minding our own business, heading home from the mall. No one was thinking, *Hey, let's get ourselves in the middle of an interstellar war.* I just wanted to get home, do all those normal things. Maybe watch TV. Check out some Web sites. Listen to a favorite CD. Do my homework.

Whatever. Normal stuff.

But the damaged Andalite fighter landed right in front of us, and from that point on, nothing was normal again.

We are not alone in this universe. There are billions of stars and billions of planets. And on some of those planets, life arose like it did here on good old Earth.

On some of those planets, highly intelligent life evolved. Just like Homo sapiens — humans — evolved here. Out there in the stars, there are races like the Ellimists who are so advanced they make humans look as dumb as cows. Then there are races, like the Andalites, more advanced than us. You know: like a tenth-grader is more advanced than an eighth-grader. But still in the same zone of reality.

And there are races like the Hork-Bajir, razor-bladed killing machines that everyone says used to be rather sweet. And the Taxxons . . . well, what can you say about the Taxxons? Huge canni-balistic centipedes. Not exactly the good guys of the galaxy. Not exactly nice.

And then there are the Yeerks.

The Yeerks, who enslaved the Hork-Bajir. The Yeerks, who made a devil's deal with the Taxxons. The Yeerks, who spread throughout the galaxy like a virus, attacking one race after another, en-slaving, destroying.

They are parasites. Just gray slugs, really. In their natural state you could step on one and squash it like a snail without its shell.

But Yeerks have the ability to infest other species. To crawl and slither and squirm inside their heads. They flatten their bodies out and wrap themselves around the brain, sinking into every crevice.

They tie into the brain. They take over the brain and enslave the poor creature, making it a Controller. They did this to Hork-Bajir and Gedds and Taxxons. All Hork-Bajir and Taxxons and Gedds are Controllers.

They've even done it to one Andalite. But only one.

Luckily.

And they are doing it to humans. Hundreds, thousands, maybe even millions of humans.

Some Controllers are taken against their will.

4

Others, believe it or not, become Controllers voluntarily.

That's always been the thing that made me maddest. Anyone can lose a battle. But to *choose* to surrender? To become a traitor? That's just sick.

The Yeerks have a front organization they call The Sharing. It's supposed to be like some kind of Boy Scouts or something, except that they take girls as well as boys, and adults as well as kids. Supposedly, it's this big family thing. You know: cookouts and rafting trips and everyone just one big, happy family.

Except that the reality is The Sharing is run by the Yeerks. They use it to learn about human society. They use it to disguise their meetings. And they use it to recruit new members.

I always wondered what lies they told people to get them to agree to become Controllers. Now I know. At least I know what it took to get one person to betray his entire planet.

I guess he betrayed me personally, too. In a way. Not that he knew me. There were probably a million girls like me with crushes on him.

I know what you're thinking. Rachel has a crush? *Rachel?* The person Marco calls *Xena: Warrior Princess*?

Well, what can I say? Cute is cute. And cuteness is a very powerful force. And he was the cutest of all cute guys that ever showed a dimple.

It was a shame I had to do what I did to him. It hurt me as much as it hurt him.

Well . . . maybe not quite as much.

But we'll get to all that grisly stuff later. I'll start at the beginning. Oddly enough, it all started at the zoo.

CHAPTER 2

"Field trip." Two of the best words in the English language. Our class was going to the zoo at The Gardens.

Sure, I'd been there before. And yes, Cassie's mom was head veterinarian, so I could get in anytime I wanted. But who cared? Any field trip was better than sitting at a desk, zoning out at a blackboard. Right? I mean, when I was younger, we went on a field trip to a factory that made bread and Twinkies. They didn't even give us any Twinkies, but did I care? No. Because being out, moving around, seeing new stuff, is always better than hard desk chairs.

Cassie didn't agree.

"*My* mom's going to give a little presentation on endangered species," Cassie said as we sauntered along with the rest of the class. "A presentation. To us."

We were in a big enclosed exhibit area. It was like a huge glass dome over all these different habitats. We were walking along at a slight downhill angle on a winding pathway between leopards and tortoises and Komodo dragons and pythons — all the animals that couldn't be exposed to cold weather.

I was enjoying myself, sipping a Mountain Dew through a straw. And checking out the occasional good-looking guy.

"Why do they even have a python exhibit?" I asked Cassie. "All they ever do is lie there. That snake might as well be fake. He could be plastic. Now, leopards, sure. They move around. They give you dirty looks. But pythons?"

"She thinks she has to be entertaining," Cassie said, still worried about her mother's presentation. "It's dangerous when Mom tries to be entertaining. See, she'll think she has to be cool and all. She'll start talking about 'The Fudgies,' or 'Snoopy Diggity Dog,' or 'Boys Eleven Men,' or 'Nice Is Neat.'"

I laughed out loud, practically spraying Mountain Dew from my nose. "Okay, The Fugees,

Snoop Doggy Dogg and Boyz II Men I get. But what's Nice Is Neat?"

Cassie looked guilty. "NIN. You know, Nine Inch Nails? I wanted to get the new CD but I was broke, so I told my mom NIN stood for Nice Is Neat."

I grabbed Cassie's arm and turned her around. "No way. *You?* That sounds like something Marco would have thought up."

Cassie quickly looked down at the ground. Then she started laughing. "Okay, it *was* Marco's idea. He said, 'What parent can possibly resist a rock group named Nice Is Neat?' See, Marco wanted me to get the CD so he could make a tape. . . . Anyway, it worked."

"Cassie, Cassie, Cassie. When you start taking advice from *Marco*, the end of civilization is very near. Besides, you and Nine Inch Nails? Do you even like the band?"

Cassie made a face. "Actually they're a little depressed and grim and harsh for me. Although it would be perfect for my mood today."

Cassie shook her head, worried again. "I know she's going to bring it up. She's going to say something like, 'Saving endangered species is cool — like listening to Nice Is Neat.' I'll have to change schools. I'll have to move to another town."

9

She grabbed my Mountain Dew and took a swig. "Why, Rachel? Why, of all the places we could go on a field trip? Why do we have to come to my mom's work?"

We leaned against the railing above the crocodile pit. About half the class had wandered on ahead. About half were still behind us. And now we were mixed in with a class of yammering, noisy kindergartners, all wearing name tags.

"I don't know," I said to Cassie. "Just your bad luck, I —" Right in front of me, not ten feet away, some dumb little boy was climbing up on the railing. "Hey! Hey! Get down off there, you —"

Suddenly, he was gone.

Over the edge.

Into the crocodile pit.

CHAPTER 3

"Haaaahhhhh!"

The little boy screamed and suddenly everyone was silent.

Then, a split second later, everyone was yelling. Me, Cassie, adults, the teachers and parent volunteers with the kindergarten.

"Help! Help!"

"He just fell in!"

"I couldn't stop him!"

"I didn't even see!"

"Tyler! Tyler! Are you all right?"

Cassie grabbed my arm to get my attention. She stared into my eyes, making sure I heard her. "I'll get help. I'll be right back. Don't do anything dumb, Rachel. *Don't!*" She sprinted away.

I leaned far out over the railing. Everyone was pushing to get a view of the kid named Tyler. But no one could see him. He had fallen straight down and rolled into a shallow alcove at the base of the wall.

The way the habitat was set up, there was a sort of island in the middle. Around it was a moat or stream or whatever you want to call it. Just below me, at the bottom of the wall, was a second dry area. I guess that's where the crocodiles went when they didn't want people staring at them.

There were six crocodiles in that pit. All six were lying peacefully on the center island, surrounded by the water. They had all been sleeping. They'd been as still and boring as the sleeping python.

But now I saw one crocodile eye open. It was a large brown eye with a black slit for a pupil. It was a sly, ruthless eye.

If the crocodiles moved for the kid, it would all be over long before help could come.

Another croc opened his eye and turned his head toward the boy.

"Oh, man," I groaned. I took a deep breath. I didn't have any morph that could take on a fifteen-foot-long crocodile. Not my grizzly bear morph. Not even my elephant morph, probably. And even to save a life, I couldn't morph in public.

Which just left two choices. Do nothing, and

let the crocodile hurt the kid. Or do something really dumb.

I chose dumb.

"Look! Over there!" I screamed as loud as I could, pointing wildly.

Every head turned to look. I jumped onto the railing, balanced myself like the amateur gymnast I am, then leaped for the branch of a fake, concrete tree overhanging the pit.

I grabbed the branch. Just like the uneven parallel bars, only it tore at my palms. I swung, then dropped to a lower branch.

I scraped my right forearm bloody, but I caught the branch, killed my speed, and dropped the last ten feet to the floor of the crocodile pit.

"Oh my God! That girl fell in, too!"

"No, she's trying to save the boy!"

"Don't be a fool!" someone yelled.

Too late, I thought grimly. I was standing on sand. The boy was behind me, sheltered from sight. Six feet of water separated me and the boy from the six crocodiles. They were all awake now. Interested. Not sure whether they should come on over and eat us or not.

And that's when I saw the reason they were unsure.

See, there weren't six crocs in the exhibit. There were seven. The seventh was lying just inches away. And he was large.

13

Large enough that if this big monster didn't want to share his prey, the other crocodiles were not going to make him mad by trying.

He was huge.

Oh, man, was he huge.

"Nice crocodile," I whispered.

He stared at me with brown-yellow eyes that almost seemed to be laughing. Of course he was laughing. He'd thought he only had one human to chomp. Now he had two.

Then he charged.

You wouldn't think something that big, with those stubby little legs, could move that fast. But he was on us like lightning! Straight at me!

I jumped in the air as that horrible snout snapped at the space where I'd been. I landed on the croc's back, fell, then scrambled wildly to get back atop him. His tail lashed like a bullwhip. He squirmed violently, trying to throw me off. His huge, gaping jaws reached back, daring me to come in range of his sharp, uneven, snaggly teeth.

I had one tiny hope. Just one. I hugged his horned, rough back, and pressed my palms against him and focused my mind with all my willpower.

I began to acquire the crocodile.

Before he could "acquire" me.

CHAPTER 4

"Acquiring." That's what we call it when we absorb the DNA of a creature.

I acquired the crocodile, absorbing the animal's DNA into my own system, making it a part of me. And, as usually happens during the acquiring, the animal became calm and peaceful.

The crocodile's tail stopped lashing. It stopped trying to throw me off. But it turned its head and glared at me with one mean eye. And I knew the peace would not last long.

But something else was happening at the same time. For the first time ever, I felt sick to my stomach while acquiring the crocodile. Sick, like I'd swallowed some spoiled milk or some-

15

thing. And at the same time, I felt a swarm of heat prickles all over my skin.

But a queasy stomach and nerves were the least of my problems.

I rolled off the croc into the alcove beside the boy. There was a bloody gash on his forehead. He was unconscious, but starting to stir and moan.

In seconds, the acquiring calm would wear off and the big crocodile would be back. His front teeth were within a foot of the boy.

From up above I could hear shouts and cries. People were rushing to help. But they wouldn't arrive in time. They couldn't even see us in the shelter of the alcove.

"Okay, Rachel," I whispered. "Focus. Do this fast!"

I felt the changes begin almost immediately. And I saw them happen. I saw the skin on my arms turn a yellowish green, then a darker, almost black-green. My skin began to crack. You know how the bottom of a dried-out lake looks? Where the mud cracks and forms big, irregular patches? That was my skin. Patterns of cracks raced across my arms and up and down my back.

I could feel the skin growing hard and crusty all along my back. It was softer, but still stiff all down my front. It didn't hurt — morphing never really hurts — but there were still things I could feel. The thickening, hardening, and cracking of my skin. The way my spine stretched and stretched, longer and longer, making little strained-bungee-cord noises. The shortening of my arms and legs.

My legs quickly grew so short I couldn't stand any longer. I fell forward, facedown in the sand.

The big crocodile was staring. At me now, rather than the little boy.

The little boy was coming to. His eyes fluttered. He moved his hands and legs. And as he moved, I could see the big crocodile's eyes focus back on him. Back on his prey.

Then my face bulged out. Out and out and out, like some awful pimple. My teeth and gums itched incredibly as new teeth appeared and old teeth grew long.

Soon I could see my own green scaly snout pushing out ahead of me. It was unbelievably long, and already I could sense the incredible power of those jaws.

Okay, Rachel, get ready! I warned myself.

I knew what was coming next. As the physical changes were completed, the crocodile mind would appear.

It's part of morphing. The mind and instincts of the animal exist right along with your own mind and thoughts. And sometimes they can be terribly hard to control.

Sometimes, control is almost impossible.

The crocodile brain didn't rush at me. It didn't do anything quickly. It was slow. So slow.

But it was slow the way a supertanker may be moving slowly, but still be impossible to stop. It rolled toward me: utter simplicity. No complex thoughts. No doubts. Just hunger. Only hunger.

I felt it bubbling up inside my own head, like a slow-motion volcano.

Resist!

But the crocodile mind had evolved millions of years before the first monkeys had swung in the trees. The crocodile mind had survived, unchanged, while dinosaurs went down to extinction and the first birds flew. It was old. Old and simple and clear, and it rolled across me, sweeping aside my fragile human thoughts.

The crocodile knew two things. There was prey — the little boy. And there was an enemy — the other big crocodile.

My eyes looked out of the sides of my head. It was good, clear vision, not much different than my own. I could see almost all around me at once. Just behind me, to my left, something struggled and moaned. I could practically taste the blood in its veins. I could sense its heat.

Just ahead of me was a big male crocodile. Just like me. He was stalking the same prey.

Simple equation: two crocodiles of equal size

stalking the same prey. I either had to fight the other croc, or lunge for the prey before the enemy could act, or back away.

I spun left, fast as a snake!

I opened my jaws so wide that my own snout hid part of the prey from view. In a second I would close my jaws on that squirming, moaning little boy and . . .

Sudden movement! I was being attacked!

The big crocodile rushed at me with amazing speed. I whipped my tail and turned to meet him. The momentum carried me off the sandbar into the water. Water! Now we could really move!

The other crocodile dived, trying to get below me to rip open my soft underbelly. I squirmed and rolled. A tail lashed through the murky water. I snapped.

Yes! My jaws closed on something and squeezed.

Then, pain! A sudden searing pain in my left hind leg. There was blood in the water. The other croc had my leg. I had his tail. We churned the water to foam, rolling and tightening our jaws.

Slowly, slowly, like I was climbing up out of a well, I felt my own mind, the mind of Rachel, start to emerge again.

I was too stunned and exhausted by the battle to resist the crocodile's cunning. It had the

19

power of total focus. It had the power of utter simplicity. It killed, it ate, and it didn't care about anything else.

We rolled insanely in the shallow water, two genetically identical crocodiles fighting a battle for dominance. Fighting to see whose mighty jaws would close on the human child.

I saw flashes of horrified onlookers up above. I saw flashes of the child starting to crawl away. I saw flashes of the other crocodiles, slithering toward the water. They hoped to take the child while the two bigger crocs were busy fighting.

I needed to win this fight to stay alive. And I needed to do it quickly to save the little boy.

I did the thing the crocodile couldn't do very well. I thought. I used my intelligence.

I let go of the tail at the same second I pulled my hind leg forward with all my strength. It was a slingshot effect. The enemy crocodile shot backward, I saw his pale belly go by, and I struck hard and fast.

He rolled away, defeated. I slewed to my right, cutting off the crocodiles who were heading for the boy. Then I raced for the sand and motored up into the alcove, out of sight of the crowd above. The boy backed away in terror.

I had no choice. I had to take a chance. I spoke to the little boy in thought-speak.

<Hey, kid! I'm the good crocodile, all right? Climb on my back!>

Fortunately, he was a cool little kid. Small enough not to question the fact that a crocodile was talking to him.

He climbed on my back like I was a pony. I slithered to the water and carried him across to the pile of fake rocks where he could climb to safety. Crocodiles can do lots of things, but they can't climb.

I raced back to the alcove and morphed back to human just as half a dozen zoo trainers armed with tranquilizer dart rifles and nets came rushing in.

The kid was safe. I was safe. Even the big croc was okay after some surgery.

So, all in all, it turned out to be a pretty cool field trip. And we never did have to hear Cassie's mom give her presentation.

CHAPTER 5

"I see," Jake said. "So basically you're saying it was no big deal. You jump into an alligator pit, you —"

"Crocodile, not alligator," Cassie corrected him.

Jake cocked one eyebrow at Cassie and she fell silent.

"You jump into a *crocodile* pit, morph into a crocodile, engage in a battle to see who's going to eat the kid, end up carrying the kid on your back, and your feeling is this was all pretty cool?"

I shrugged and looked to Cassie for support.

"She *did* save the kid," Cassie pointed out.

"She also came very, very close to showing the

entire world what she really is," Jake said, using the low, silky voice he uses when he's really upset.

After saving the kid, you'd think my friends would have welcomed me as a hero, right? Wrong.

Here's the scene. Me, Cassie, Jake, Marco, Tobias, and Ax were all in Cassie's barn, which is also the Wildlife Rehabilitation Clinic. So picture cages everywhere, stuffed with every kind of injured, sick, messed-up raccoon, squirrel, duck, wild pig, bat, skunk, fox, eagle, and deer.

Jake was pacing back and forth, which he also does when he's upset. Jake isn't a yelling kind of person when he's mad. He's a grinding-his-teeth, pacing, and talking-in-a-low-silky-voice kind of person.

Jake is in charge, more or less. No one exactly elected him, but if we ever did vote on it he'd get all the votes — except his own. There was just never any question who was going to be the leader. Probably because we all know Jake isn't the kind of person who really *wants* to be a boss. He does it because someone has to, not because it makes him feel important.

I would probably think Jake was good-looking. Except that he's my cousin. But of course Cassie thinks he's perfect. Cassie and Jake have a little *thing* going. Neither of them admits it, of course. And they never really say anything to each other

23

about it. They think no one else knows. But they have a definite thing. Trust me.

Anyway, lounging on a big bale of hay was Marco. Marco is Jake's best friend. Marco is not the leadership type. He's very smart but unfortunately, he uses all his brain to make stupid jokes.

Okay, maybe not all his brain. If he used *all* his brain to make jokes, the jokes would probably be better.

Marco is cute, although not as cute as he thinks he is. See, it would be impossible for anyone to be as cute as Marco thinks he is. Marco's ego is totally out of control.

Then, there is Tobias. He was up in the rafters overhead, carefully combing his feathers with his beak.

Tobias is what the Andalites call a *nothlit*. That means a person who is trapped in a morph. There's a two-hour time limit on morphing. Stay more than two hours and you stay forever.

Tobias used to be this kind of dweebish kid with crazed blond hair and a dreamy expression. But now he is a red-tailed hawk. The dreamy expression is long gone. It's been replaced by the laser-intensity stare of a raptor.

Tobias has had to accept the fact that he is not fully human anymore. Inside, he's still Tobias. But he lives in the woods and hunts for his food, and that has changed him.

Then there is Cassie. Cassie is my best friend, although we're nothing alike. Cassie is probably the most capable, in-charge, amazing person I will ever meet. This is a girl who deals with school, has practically a full-time job helping her dad with the Wildlife Rehabilitation Clinic, and handles all the stuff we have to deal with as Animorphs. I mean, who else can keep up a *B-plus* average while she's saving wild animals and fighting a war with the Yeerk empire?

Last, and definitely weirdest, is Ax. His full name is Aximili-Esgarrouth-Isthill. Which is why we just call him "Ax." He doesn't usually come to meetings, because he has to travel in human morph. He doesn't like going into human morph because he thinks walking around on just two legs is dangerous.

Since we were safe inside the barn, Ax was back in his own body now. His body is a strange but cool-looking mix of bluish deer body, human-like arms and shoulders, and definitely alien head. He has no mouth. He has two big, seminormal eyes on his face where eyes should be, and two extra eyes stuck on short stalks on top of his head.

And he has a tail. Like a scorpion's tail. Very fast, very dangerous in a fight.

Normally when we're in the barn, Cassie would be busily cleaning cages or giving medications to skanky lizards or whatever. But I guess she felt like she had to help me defend myself. So she was standing there, looking guilty even though she hadn't done anything wrong.

"What was I supposed to do?" I asked Jake. "Let the little boy get chomped?"

"Yes!" Marco said, speaking up. "Yes. See, we're fighting to save the *whole* world, not one kid. And you endangered all that by trying to be the offspring of *Xena: Warrior Princess* and Superman."

<Xena and Superman have a child? I didn't even know they were dating,> Tobias said in open thought-speak.

I smiled up at him. He couldn't smile back, of course.

Then, in a whisper that only I could hear, Tobias added, <Rachel. Ask Jake what he would have done. That'll get him off your back.>

I carefully avoided nodding or giving any sign that Tobias had whispered to me. "Jake, if you think what I did was so wrong, what would *you* have done?"

Jake stopped pacing. "The point is, secrecy is absolutely important," he said.

"Jake," I repeated, "what would you have done in my place?"

CHAPTER 6

Jake scratched his ear. He grinned sheepishly. "Just because I would have done the same thing doesn't make it right."

"I think Rachel was a real hero," Cassie said.

<Rachel was brave. Bravery is a great virtue.>

Marco rolled his eyes at Ax. "Thank you, Obi-Wan Kenobi, for that wisdom. Of *course* she was a hero. She's *always* a hero. Rachel can't stop being heroic. Being stupidly brave is like some nervous tic she can't control. But what if someone had caught her morphing on videotape?"

That wiped the smile off my face. As much as Marco annoyed me, he was right. If someone had taped me . . . the Yeerks are everywhere. If they'd had evidence I'd morphed a crocodile they would know who and what I was.

The Yeerks believe we are a highly trained group of Andalite warriors. If they ever found out we were just human kids . . . we'd be wiped out before we could blink twice.

"Okay, well, anyway, Rachel, you were very brave. You were also very lucky. The news reports say you 'fell into' the pit because you were trying to see the kid. Everyone is focused on how amazing it supposedly was that a kid could ride an alligator . . . crocodile. The kid's going to be on five different talk shows."

"Great. So I'm the idiot girl who 'fell' into the pit, and the kid is some big hero."

"Be glad it worked out that well," Jake said.

For a moment, I considered mentioning the way I'd felt sick while morphing the crocodile. But I decided against it. Why give Jake anything else to worry about?

Cassie raised her hand. "Are we done with yelling at Rachel? I have work to do."

Jake laughed. "I don't yell," he said. "I'm not anyone's parent."

"You tell 'em, Dad," Marco said.

We all laughed and the tension was broken. For about ten seconds — till Jake said, "Hey, by the way, Tom said something about how The

Sharing is going to hire that kid from *Power House* as a spokesman."

"That TV show?" Marco said. "Huh. That's strange. Well, anyway, I have homework piled up on my desk at home. Plus, I have the new Nintendo game. You know, the one where —"

He stopped talking and just stared at Cassie and me. Probably because Cassie and I were standing there with our mouths hanging open.

"What's with them?" Marco asked Jake.

Jake looked mystified. "What *is* with you two?"

"Jeremy Jason McCole is going to be endorsing The Sharing?" I asked in a wavering voice.

"Jeremy Jason McCole?" Cassie echoed in awestruck tones.

Jake shrugged. "Yeah, it's too bad, but it's not like anyone cares. He's just some wimpy little actor. I mean, it's not like he's Michael Jordan . . ."

". . . or Brett Favre," Marco added.

< . . . or Wayne Gretzky,> Tobias offered.

<What is an actor?> Ax wondered.

". . . or anyone else important," Jake concluded. "He's just an actor. I mean, he's a dork."

<What is a dork?> Ax asked.

<That hair!> Tobias said derisively.

"I *love* his hair," Cassie said.

"Plus he's even shorter than I am," Marco said.

29

"The difference being that Jeremy Jason Mc-Cole is cute," I said.

"He's more than cute," Cassie said. "He is the single cutest boy on the planet."

"He's in every magazine," I said. "*Teen, YM, Seventeen.*"

"*Wussy Weekly, Midget Monthly, The New Dork Times . . .*" Marco added. He and Jake exchanged a high five.

I ignored Marco. I almost always do. Instead I made sure Jake was paying attention, and I said, "Jake, you're not getting it. About half the girls in our school have a poster of Jeremy Jason Mc-Cole in their bedrooms or in their lockers, or both. He is the number one cute guy in the country. He has like twenty Web sites just about him. If he endorses The Sharing, it would be as if . . ." I looked to Cassie for help.

"As if the entire female cast of *Baywatch* endorsed something," Cassie supplied.

"Yeah. Like that."

Jake's smile evaporated. "You're saying this actor kid has that kind of influence?"

"He has that much power?" Marco said. "He has *Baywatch*-level power?"

<Yasmine Bleeth power?> Tobias echoed.

<Bleeth?> Ax echoed. <Is that a word?>

"If Jeremy Jason McCole becomes a spokesman for The Sharing, they'll be signing up girls like crazy," I said.

"Then this is serious," Jake said.

"Yeah, Jake, it is. We have to stop this from happening."

Cassie sent me a sly, sidelong glance. "Of course . . . we might have to actually *meet* Jeremy Jason in order to save him."

"We have to do our duty," I said. "I mean, for a start, we have to find out if he's already a Controller."

"And we'd probably have to meet him to do that."

"Get close to him."

"Very close."

"Absolutely."

"Mmm-hmmm."

"The two of you are making me sick," Jake said.

CHAPTER 7

Reruns of *Power House* came on every night at seven. Just after the news. I watched it with my two little sisters, Sara and Jordan. Sara was too little to care one way or the other about boys. But Jordan was closer to my age.

"You think Jeremy Jason McCole is cute?" I asked her.

"On a scale of one to ten? Maybe about a thousand."

I nodded. "Yeah. He is cute."

"He's even cuter than that guy Marco. You know the one who's Cousin Jake's friend?"

"Yeah, I know Marco," I said cautiously. I shuddered. "You actually think Marco is cute?"

"Sure."

"Jordan, do me and the whole world a favor. Never, ever tell him."

"As if!"

"But you don't think he's as cute as Jeremy Jason, right?"

"Of course not. Jeremy Jason is famous."

"Oh. Well, let me ask you something. If you thought there was some club you could belong to that would mean you might get to meet Jeremy Ja —"

She leaped up. "What club? What club? What *club*?!"

Which answered my question. I wasn't foolish enough to worry about what might happen if Jeremy Jason McCole came out in support of The Sharing. If anything, I wasn't worrying enough.

If using Jeremy Jason worked at recruiting girls into The Sharing, what would the Yeerks do next?

I watched *Power House* with a whole new outlook, knowing what I now knew about one of its stars. Was it really possible that someone like Jeremy Jason McCole could be a Controller?

No way. And if I did just happen to save him from being taken by the Yeerks. Well . . .

After dinner and after *Power House*, I went up to my room to attack my backed-up homework. I had a paper due and it was supposed to be five pages long, at least. I had maybe four pages worth of material. So I played with fonts and

33

margins until my four pages could more or less fill five pages. Then I hit "print" and hoped my teacher wouldn't figure out what I'd done.

"Rachel? I'm running down to the store for some milk," my mom yelled up the stairs. "You're in charge."

I dropped out of the word-processing program and logged on to the Internet. I opened my window since it was a warm night out and Tobias sometimes flew by in the evening.

Then I started checking out the various Web sites for Jeremy Jason.

"Know your enemy," I muttered under my breath. Not that I could really think of Jeremy Jason as my enemy.

I had to wait through several busy signals to reach his own actual home page. My screen filled with a picture of the actor.

"Way too cute to be a Controller," I said to no one.

I scrolled down and found a button for his biography. It was two pages long. I printed it out. Then I clicked on his schedule of appearances. It was slightly out-of-date. I scrolled down the page. Then, "Whoa! Whoa!"

I stopped and scrolled back. There it was. The twenty-fourth. Jeremy Jason was doing the *Barry and Cindy Sue Show* on the road. On the road . . . right in our town for the week.

Two days from now! He's going to be here! Here!

I snatched up the portable phone. I speed-dialed Cassie. "He's coming here!"

"Who? What?"

"Jeremy Jason. He's going to be on the *Barry and Cindy Sue Show* when they come to town!"

"No way!"

"Oh, yes. Definitely yes." I hung up and started to click to another Web site to confirm the news.

I felt like I couldn't breathe. I was majorly excited. I know, I know, it isn't really cool to get all mental about a TV actor, but Jeremy Jason Mc-Cole was like my first crush going back to when I was ten.

I took a deep, steadying breath.

But I couldn't quite do it. My breathing was short. Rough. Like I was being squeezed. A swarming feeling of heat needles spread across my skin.

This wasn't about Jeremy Jason. There was definitely something wrong with me. I couldn't breathe!

I sucked in air and pushed myself back from the computer.

And that's when I noticed my hand.

My right hand was green. A dark, mottled, reptile green.

CHAPTER 8

"What the . . ."

I held up my left hand. It was green, too. Getting greener as I watched. Getting rougher. Changing. Morphing!

There were scales forming on my skin. Crawling up my arms.

I bolted from the chair and raced for my full-length mirror.

My face was just beginning to bulge out. A huge, long, black-green snout.

This is something you never want to actually see.

"Yahhhh!" I yelped.

The swelling bulge split open to reveal a row of long, yellowed teeth.

"Crckkk!" I started to say, but my mouth was no longer human enough to make human sounds.

My legs shriveled as I watched helplessly. I fell forward onto the floor. The huge tail was surging behind me. I felt my spine stretching.

No! No! I hadn't decided to morph!

And yet I was morphing. At warp speed! I was on the floor of my bedroom, turning into a murderous, twenty-foot-long crocodile.

Morph out! I ordered myself. *Morph out!*

But the transformation continued. I was too big for the room! My snout was pushed into one corner, while my tail stretched out under the bed and curled in the far corner.

What was happening to me?

If Jordan or Sara or my mother walked into the room, my secret would be out. Worse yet, I wasn't sure I could control the crocodile.

It was hungry.

Focus, Rachel! Focus! Morph out! Go human!

But I wasn't morphing out. At least, not back to human.

Instead I began to notice a completely different kind of change. My body was narrowing in two places. I was cinching up. Forming three different body sections: head, abdomen, and thorax.

I was becoming an insect!

37

And that's when I became afraid. See, it's impossible to morph straight from one animal to another. Or at least it's *supposed* to be impossible. But I was definitely morphing. And I was not morphing to human.

I was still a huge crocodile, but my massive crocodile head was connected to my body by a tiny, narrow neck. And the area connecting my squat crocodile body to my fat crocodile tail had narrowed so much it was the size of a human wrist.

<This can't be happening!> I cried to no one. <This has to be a dream.>

But I'd had dozens, maybe hundreds of awful morphing dreams. And they'd never been like this.

I could hear my bones squishing as they turned to water and disappeared. I could see the black-green crocodile scales turn dark brown, almost black, as an insect's exoskeleton grew over me like armor.

Huge spiky hairs shot like daggers from my back. My big teeth melted together, solidified, blackened, and reformed to become a long, vile-looking tube. Two new legs spurted from my sides. Two spiky, multi-jointed legs.

I knew all these changes. This was a morph I had done before. But never like this!

I was on my way to becoming a fly. But because morphing is never logical, I was a gigantic fly. I was becoming a fly before I'd had a chance to shrink.

Then the shrinkage kicked in and I was spiraling wildly downward. I was going from twenty-five feet in length to less than a quarter of an inch!

I wanted to scream for help. But who could help me? No one. No one!

Suddenly my reptile eyes bulged and popped out like balloons. The world around me was shattered into a thousand tiny pictures. I had the compound eyes of a fly!

My mind was reeling. It had to be a nightmare. This wasn't possible. It had to be some awful dream!

I was shrinking so fast that the corners of the room seemed to be racing away from me. The wood grain grew large and dark and clear. The cracks between boards were growing as wide as ditches.

And then, with a sickening lurch, I realized I had stopped shrinking. I was growing again.

The wood grain grew smaller. The cracks shrank. And I grew. And grew. And grew!

My extra legs were gone. I had just four now. Four legs growing thicker and taller and thicker and taller!

<Oh, please! Someone help me!>

Sproing! Sproing! The springs in my mattress popped as my bulk crushed them. I was too big for the room. Bigger even than the crocodile. My bookshelves fell over. My desk slammed against the wall. Sparks shot from my computer and the screen went blank.

Too big for the room! I was big enough to be weighed in tons, not pounds. I was morphing a full-grown African elephant. In my small bedroom.

C-r-r-r-r-r-e-e-e-e-k!

<Oh, no,> I whispered. I could feel the floor literally sinking under my impossible weight. My head was shoved up against the ceiling.

C-r-r-r-UNCH!

With a scream of twisting wood, the floor gave way.

A sickening drop! And . . .

C-r-r-a-BOOOOM!

I was, very suddenly, in the kitchen.

CHAPTER 9

CRASH!
CRUNCH!

I staggered and fell against the rubble of my room and the even bigger mess of the kitchen. It was chaos! Nothing made any sense.

The stove sat at a ridiculous angle with a two-by-four piece of lumber spearing through its glass door. The refrigerator was open, with all its contents spilled out. A gallon of milk glub-glubbed all over the place.

Sara! Jordan! Had they been in the kitchen? Had my mom?

Oh, God! No one could have survived being crushed under this mess!

"Rachel! Rachel!"

It was Jordan's voice. She sounded scared but okay. And my elephant ears told me she was not in the room with me. She was out in the hallway. She couldn't see me through the rubble.

I couldn't answer. I didn't have a human mouth or throat.

Could I get out of morph? I had to try.

I focused my mind on my own body. My human self. And slowly at first, then faster, I began to shrink.

Suddenly the boards and Sheetrock were no longer pressing in so tightly around me. In the hallway I could hear Jordan saying, "Nine-one-one? Um, um, we have an emergency! Our house fell in!"

I would have laughed . . . if I'd been sure Sara and my mother were both safe. Then I remembered — my mother was out. That just left Sara.

Meanwhile, I began to see the best sight in the world: human flesh emerging from the thick gray skin of the elephant. I was still on all fours, but I could see fingers beginning to grow from the massive elephant feet.

"Rachel! Rachel, where are you?"

Sara's voice this time. She must have taken the phone. I breathed a huge sigh of relief.

"Yes, get here right away! Please! I think my sister is trapped!"

My trunk slurped up into my face, leaving my tiny human nose behind. I cleared my throat. Could I talk yet?

"Jordan?" I said. Yes. It was my voice. My own human voice!

"Rachel? Is that you?"

"Well, who else would it be?" I asked. I didn't mean to sound sarcastic. I was scared half to death, and I get snippy when I'm scared.

"That's Rachel, all right," Sara said.

"Are you okay?"

"I'm bruised up," I said. "But I guess I'll live."

Had I been in human form when the floor collapsed, I'd have been dead or on my way to a long stay in a hospital for sure. On the other hand, if I'd been human, the floor wouldn't have collapsed in the first place.

What was happening to me? Why in the heck had I morphed?

I had a few minutes to think that over while the paramedics and fire department and police and my mom and every person within six blocks showed up. But there were no answers.

I had morphed without wanting to.

The fire department guys dug me out of the rubble. They kept telling me not to worry. What did they know? Had they ever suddenly turned into a crocodile? Had they ever had uncontrolled morphing?

My mom was home by the time they dug me out. She did a lot of yelling and wailing and hugging and crying. They made me take an ambulance to the hospital to be checked over.

It was total *E.R.* for a while. I told them I was fine, but no one could believe it. No one could believe that a girl could be trapped in a collapsed house and still be unhurt.

Then the TV stations found out I was the same girl who had "fallen" into the crocodile pit. So for about an hour after that I had to answer really stupid questions from reporters who shoved cameras and lights in my face.

I sat there on the hospital bed, wearing the black leotard I wear for morphing, entirely surrounded by microphones being jabbed at me. I just kept thinking, *Man, my hair is probably a mess.*

"How did it feel to fall into a crocodile pit, then have your house fall down on you?"

"Not very good," I answered.

"Don't you think you're incredibly lucky?"

"Um, no. If I were lucky I wouldn't keep falling. Right?"

"But you weren't hurt either time."

"I think winning the lottery would be lucky.

Having the house fall on me, that's not all that lucky."

Behind the cameras I saw a familiar face. Cassie. The two of us locked eyes. All I could do was shrug.

"Do you have any advice for other kids like yourself?"

"Um, yes. My advice is don't fall into crocodile pits and don't have the house fall on you."

After that, the news people decided I was being sarcastic, I guess. They decided they'd had enough. Which was good, because I'd definitely had enough.

"Sweetheart, are you okay?" my mom asked for about the millionth time once all the cameras were gone.

Cassie was right beside her. "Yeah, how are you?" she asked in a carefully neutral voice.

I shrugged. "I'm fine. I'd be even more fine if I weren't suddenly 'The Amazing Falling Girl.'" Unfortunately, my mom was not one of the people I could talk to openly about what had happened. Cassie was. But that would have to wait till we were alone.

My mother laughed and ruffled my hair. "You *are* amazing, Rachel. It's a miracle you survived. I think we should all be thankful."

"Thankful? The house fell on me. The house is destroyed."

"We have insurance," my mom said. Then she grinned. "Plus we probably have the mother of all lawsuits. I mean, houses shouldn't fall apart like that. We can go after the builder, all the contractors and subcontractors, the city inspectors, the previous owners, the . . ."

She went on like that for a while. See, my mom is a lawyer.

"Can we get out of here now?"

"The doctors say you're okay. But the question is, where do we go? We can't go back to the house and —"

"Daddy!"

I caught sight of him looming up behind Cassie. My parents are divorced. My dad lives in another state now, but I get to see him once a month. Most months, anyway.

"Hi, Dan," my mom said in the fake-nice voice she uses with my dad.

"Hello, Naomi," he said in his version of the fake-nice voice. Then in a genuine voice he said, "How's my girl?"

I shrugged. "No biggie, Dad. The usual day: a little crocodile-diving in the morning, then the house falls in on me."

He laughed. My dad is very cool. He's a TV reporter himself. But not like the ones who'd been driving me crazy. My dad is more like one of those *60 Minutes* guys. You know, like very responsible and serious.

At least on TV he's serious. In regular life, he's not that way at all.

"I saw the report on the thing at the zoo," he said. "I caught the next flight. It never occurred to me you'd be performing another bizarre stunt the same day."

"Yeah, well, that's it for this week, though," I said. "I figure that's about enough excitement."

He laughed and my mom rolled her eyes. She thinks I like my father better than her. That's not true at all. Not really. It's just that my mom is always around. Unlike my dad.

"Where are you all going to stay?" he asked my mother.

"At my mom's, I guess," she said. Under her breath she added, "until the old woman drives me stark raving nuts."

My dad nodded in sympathy. "Look, I'm staying in town for a couple of days. I thought maybe I'd run interference for Rachel. Keep the media off her."

"They seem to have given up on this story," my mother said doubtfully.

My dad shook his head. "Don't count on it. They were just trying to make their deadlines for the late news. This is a good human-interest story. But as a fellow reporter I might be able to warn some of them off."

"Rachel can stay with me," Cassie said. "I know my mom and dad wouldn't mind."

My father winked at her. "Thanks, Cassie." Then he turned back to me. "Look, Rachel, I have a suite at the Fairview Hotel. Why not stay with me till this all blows over? Room service? Health club?"

"Cool! I mean, is it okay, Mom?"

She looked grumpy. "Well, it makes sense. I guess."

Right then, I realized that a wonderful, perfect, golden opportunity had just opened up right in front of me.

"Dad? What you said about all the talk shows wanting to interview me? Wouldn't it be better if I agreed to do just one show? Then the others would let me be. Right?"

He nodded. "Yeah. But, sweetie, you don't have to do *any* show. I can get everyone off your back."

"I could do one, though," I said. "In fact . . . what do you think of the *Barry and Cindy Sue Show*? I heard they were coming to town."

Both my parents looked confused. But I saw realization dawn in Cassie's eyes.

"*Barry and Cindy Sue*?" my mom said.

"Rachel, why exactly would you want to do *Barry and Cindy Sue*?"

I saw Cassie just staring at me with her jaw hanging open. Like she couldn't believe I was even thinking about the whole Jeremy Jason Mc-Cole thing at a time like this.

"Well, Daddy . . . there's this guy. This actor . . . this kind of slightly cute actor . . ."

CHAPTER 10

I went straight from the hospital to my dad's hotel. Everyone had decided I needed rest. I didn't. What I did need was some answers.

What was happening to me?

The hotel room was on the twenty-second floor. I imagined what would happen if I suddenly morphed an elephant again. I'd crash down through twenty-two floors.

What on Earth was happening to me? I kept checking my hands and feet to see if I was still totally human.

I needed to talk to someone who understood. Someone I could really talk to. My dad was great, but he just kept talking about how the floor shouldn't just fall in. After all, the house was only ten years old. And while they were at it, why didn't the zoo make its railings higher so people wouldn't be falling in with the crocodiles?

I hadn't fallen into the croc pit. And the floor didn't just happen to collapse. I had morphed an animal that weighed more than a couple of pickup trucks. Houses aren't made for elephants.

I desperately wanted to call Cassie and talk to her on the phone. But we have a strict rule about that. You never know who is listening in on a phone call. So it would just have to wait.

Instead I called room service.

"I'd like a salad with the poppyseed dressing. And, um . . . I'd like the cheeseburger and fries. And cherry pie à la mode. And cancel the salad."

I didn't care about eating healthy. I didn't care about fat. I was hungry. It had been a long, bad day. I deserved some grease and sugar.

"And do you make milk shakes? Chocolate milk shakes?"

I used the remote control to run through the Pay-Per-View choices. It was nothing but martial arts movies, crime movies, action–adventure movies. . . . What I needed was a nice, calm romance. My *life* was an action–adventure movie.

The phone rang. I expected it to be the room service people checking back. "Yes?"

51

"Are you alone?" It was Cassie's voice. I nearly collapsed from relief. I hadn't even realized how incredibly tense I was.

"I'm so glad it's you! Yes, my dad's gone. At least for a couple hours."

"Does your window open?"

I got up and checked. The window slid open easily. "Yes. You coming up?"

"Give me five minutes. Flick the lights a couple of times so I know which window is you."

I spent the five minutes calling down to room service and ordering the salad again. And another piece of pie. For Cassie.

I was expecting her, but I was still a little startled when a great horned owl came flying in through the window.

<All clear?> Cassie asked anxiously.

"Yeah. But hurry up and morph out. Room service is coming."

Morphing is never pretty to watch. In fact, it can be the most horrible thing in the world. If you weren't expecting it, and just saw it happening for the first time, I promise you'd run screaming like a lunatic.

Especially some morphs. Trust me, you don't ever want to see a person become a fly or a spider. You think you've seen scary stuff on TV or in horror movies? Hah. Watch your friend turn into a bug. That will fill your dreams for a few weeks.

But if anyone can make morphing not totally vile and horrifying, it's Cassie. Cassie has a natural talent for it. A natural ability.

So she looked almost normal as the feathers sank into her skin and disappeared. It didn't even seem too bizarre when her own legs grew huge and tall from the owl's short, deadly talons.

It was her head that changed last. Cassie has the ability to do that: sort of control the order things morph. I can't even come close. Even Ax can't do it.

Finally, the big owl eyes became Cassie's own deep, dark eyes.

There came a knock at the door. I held up a hand to calm Cassie. "It's just room service. You like pie, right?"

The waiter wheeled a small table into the room. It was loaded with my burger and Cassie's salad and two pieces of pie and my milk shake.

I signed the check and added a tip. See, I'd visited my dad in hotels before. I knew the routine pretty well.

Cassie laughed when the waiter had gone. "You're going to have to be rich when you grow up, Rachel. I mean, this is all so natural for you. You fit right in."

I grinned. "I have a natural talent for spending money. What can I say? It's my burden to bear."

Cassie got serious. "Okay. Talk to me. What happened?"

"What? You mean you don't believe that the floor of my bedroom just happened to fall in?"

She shook her head. "No."

I took a big bite of the burger, chewed, and swallowed. "I think I must have fallen asleep. I was clicking around some Web sites. . . . Suddenly, I was morphing into that big crocodile from today." I shrugged and took another bite.

"You just started morphing?"

"Yeah. I don't know . . . I mean, I *thought* I was awake. But I must have been dreaming."

"Uh-uh. I dream all the time," Cassie said. "I've never morphed in my sleep."

I didn't want to dismiss the possibility it was a dream that caused me to morph. The alternative — that I was just out of control — was worse. "Are you going to eat that salad? It cost like ten dollars."

"We all have nightmares and stuff. None of us has ever just started morphing." Cassie dug into her salad. But she was watching me all the time.

I concentrated on my burger. "What can I say? That must be what happened. I must have had a nightmare."

"And you morphed the croc and it made the floor fall in?"

I shifted nervously. "Okay, look, actually, it

was my elephant morph. See, I think what happened is that maybe I just dreamed the part about morphing the crocodile. Because then I went straight into another morph, and then . . . when I woke up . . . I was an elephant."

Cassie looked down at her plate like she was embarrassed. "Rachel. It's me, okay? Me. Cassie. Your best friend. I know when you're not telling the complete truth."

That killed off what was left of my appetite. I put the burger down. "Okay, look. I don't know what happened, all right? I was on-line, I was getting kind of logy the way I do when I'm staring at a computer screen. Then all of a sudden I'm going crocodile."

"We have to talk to Ax about this. He's an Andalite. Maybe it's some normal thing that happens sometimes."

"It better not be something that just happens," I said. "I could have killed Jordan and Sara. It was just dumb luck that they were in the living room, not the kitchen."

Cassie nodded. "Yeah. Well, we need to talk to Ax."

I reached across the table and took her hand. "But not Jake, okay? He'll just get all responsible. He won't let me do anything. He'll tell me to stay home."

"That's what you *should* do."

55

"No." I shook my head violently. "What I need is to stay focused. The more focused I am, the less likely that will ever happen again. I'm not going to *let* it happen." I really hoped that was true.

I picked up my burger. Cassie stared at me for a while, then she started picking at her salad again.

"Okay," she said after a while. "But we talk to Ax."

"Deal," I said.

"By the way. It turns out Jeremy Jason McCole is already in town."

"What?"

She nodded. Then she smiled. "It was on *Entertainment Tonight*. He's staying on this big yacht owned by some movie producer. He's out on the bay right now."

"We still need to figure out if he's already a Controller or not," I said. "I asked Jordan what she'd do if she thought there was some way she could get close to Jeremy Jason McCole. She basically said she'd walk barefoot over broken glass."

"I'm not surprised," Cassie said. "A year ago I'd probably have been right behind her." She grinned crookedly. "Love is a powerful force."

I attacked my burger again. "So? We go see

Jeremy Jason on this yacht? The movie producer guy could be a Controller."

"That's what Jake and Marco and Tobias and Ax and I already talked about. We thought tomorrow after school we'd maybe go out there and take a look."

"Jake, Marco . . . all of them? They're coming, too?"

"Somehow they don't seem to exactly trust you and me alone with Jeremy Jason."

"On a yacht, huh?" Rachel mused. "He'll probably be lying out in a bathing suit."

"Mmmm."

"Mmm-hmm."

CHAPTER 11

I woke up approximately fifty times during the night. I kept having to check to make sure I was human. And I had some seriously odd dreams. In one, I morphed into Jeremy Jason and then got fly eyes.

Not a good night's sleep. My dad came in from the next room at about four in the morning to tell me I woke him up talking in my sleep.

"You were yelling, 'Crocodile not alligator!'" he said.

Fortunately, he just figured it was stress from the insane day I'd had. He was right. But he didn't know half of it.

I took a taxi from the hotel to school. It beat

taking the bus, that's for sure. Maybe Cassie was right. Maybe I'll have to be rich when I grow up.

For the first couple of periods I had to put up with kids saying brilliant things like, "Hey! It's Crocodile Dundee!" And, "Stay away from me. You'll make the school fall down."

And then there were the people who actually seemed jealous. "I guess you think you're cool just because you nearly got killed twice in one day," one girl said.

"Yeah, that's right," I said. "Later, just to prove how cool I am, I'm going to jump off a cliff."

By the time lunch was over, most people had gotten the message that I didn't really want to talk about it.

Then I was called to the assistant principal's office.

Chapman's office.

I guess I should explain. Chapman is one of *them*. He's a high-ranking Controller. He's one of the leaders of The Sharing.

He once came very close to having me killed. Not that he knew it was me, really. But still, I kind of resented it.

I walked the empty hallway, clutching my hall pass and wondering how I was going to escape if Chapman was waiting for me with a bunch of Hork-Bajir warriors.

"Rachel, come on in, come on in. Have a seat."

Chapman looks perfectly normal. He's a little bald, but normal-looking. That's the problem with Controllers: They don't look any different.

"Um, what's this about, Mr. Chapman?" I asked nervously. I was playing the role of any normal kid who gets called to the assistant principal's office. It was easy to act nervous.

He waved his hand dismissively. "I just wanted to talk to the big celebrity."

I sat down, but I stayed tense and ready to spring into action. Did Chapman suspect? Had he figured out that I hadn't just fallen into the crocodile pit? Had he figured out that I *was* the crocodile who had carried the little boy to safety?

I was dead meat if he had. The Yeerks believe we are a group of Andalite bandits. See, they know they're getting attacked by a group of people who can morph. It just never occurs to them that humans could morph.

If they knew the truth . . . well, there's a good reason we keep the truth a secret.

"So."

"So," I agreed.

"Yesterday was quite a day for you," Chapman said.

"Yes, sir."

"You were very lucky. Twice."

"Yes. I guess so. But I guess the way I look at it, I was unlucky twice."

He nodded like I'd said something deep. "No injuries?"

I shook my head. "No."

"Amazing," he said. Then he narrowed his eyes and stared hard at me. "Rachel. Your grades have dropped this last semester. Not a lot. But your teachers think you aren't applying yourself the way you used to."

"I still have an *A* average," I pointed out.

"Barely."

I squirmed in my seat. This was insane. I wasn't sure if I was being interrogated by a dangerous Controller who suspected my true identity. Or if I was just being lectured about my grades by an assistant principal.

"Has anything changed in your life lately?"

I almost swallowed my tongue. Had anything changed? Like, for example, being given the power to morph by a dying alien and ending up fighting an invasion of Earth by parasite slugs from outer space?

"Um . . . nope," I said. "No big changes."

He smiled an understanding smile. "Your parents got divorced, didn't they? And didn't your father move away?"

I tried not to look too relieved. But I definitely sighed. "Oh, yeah. Oh, that. Um, yes. Maybe

61

that's why my grades are down a little. That must be it. You know, the trauma and all."

I felt my feet itching. It was a strange thing to notice right then, with Chapman staring at me like I was some mystery he was trying to understand. But they were definitely itching. And I was feeling flushed . . . warm all over.

"Well, as you may or may not know, Rachel, I am the local head of a wonderful group called The Sharing."

And that's when my heart stopped beating.

CHAPTER 12

My heart missed about four beats before it started up again, going a hundred miles an hour. "Uh-huh," I said, trying not to let the adrenaline rush overwhelm me.

Get ready, I told myself. *Get ready.*

"We like to think we offer some help to kids who may be going through a bad time," Chapman said. "We have an awful lot of fun. Campouts. Bonfire barbecues on the beach. Just a month or so back we had a big waterskiing trip up to a mountain lake."

I could have said, "Yes, I know. We were there, too, but not exactly in human shapes."

Instead I said, "That sounds like fun."

"It is fun," Chapman said with total sincerity.

63

"And a lot of our members are kids who come from troubled homes. Kids with problems. But they're also kids who want to make life better. They're hopeful, optimistic kids. When I saw you handling yourself so well on the news last night I thought, you know, I should offer Rachel this opportunity. She's just the kind of person who could really benefit from The Sharing."

"How did I look on TV?" I asked.

"Very self-possessed. Very attractive and very mature."

"Cool."

"But . . ." He sighed. "I have to wonder at the same time if maybe you don't have some problems in your life. I mean, the stories all say you *fell* into the crocodile pit . . ."

I held my breath. Here it comes! He suspects!

". . . but I don't believe in accidents. I have to wonder if maybe you have some problems that made you, shall we say, careless."

I barked out a laugh. Then I stopped myself. He thought I was suicidal! Did he think I'd sawed through the floor of my house, too? Good grief. That's why he was trying to recruit me for The Sharing. He thought I was depressed or whatever. A perfect recruit for his little Controller organization.

Yeah, right. Where do I sign up, Mr. Chapman? Could there be a special discount on dues for Animorphs?

I shook my head. "No. Actually, I'm very happy."

Once again, a feeling like pins and needles of warmth swarming over me. I shifted my feet. The feeling was familiar . . .

Oh, no!

Oh, no! My *feet*!

I looked down and it took every single ounce of my self-control to keep the look of horror from my face.

My feet were swelling. They were growing thick, shaggy brown fur. They were swelling and straining my shoes. The laces were strained tight.

"I know you say everything is fine, Rachel, but —"

SNAP!

He frowned. "What was that?"

SNAP!

"Nothing," I said in a squeaky voice.

"I heard something pop."

My laces had snapped from the pressure. I shook my head. "No."

"Anyway, what I was saying, was . . . Rachel? Are you listening?"

No, I wasn't listening. I was busy trying to see

if any other parts of me were turning into grizzly bear. Because, see, that's what it was. I'd seen those feet before. They were bear feet.

"Um, yes! Yes. I am listening very closely!"

Oh, please! No way! I can't morph here! Not right in Chapman's office. I focused. I concentrated. Demorph!

Chapman just kept droning on. On and on about The Sharing. And all the while, my shoes were torn to ribbons. And my legs, from the knees down, grew shaggy with long, rough brown fur. And hard nails grew where my toes had been.

"Anyway," Chapman said, suddenly glancing at his watch. "I'm going on and on. And you need to get back to class."

"What?" I asked frantically.

"Just think about it, Rachel," Chapman said. "Now, go straight back to class. No dawdling."

I gulped. What could I do?

I bent over and quickly stuffed the torn remnants of my shoes into my backpack.

My feet were like huge, fur boots.

In fact . . .

I stood up and headed for the door. I paused with my hand on the knob. I turned back and saw Chapman staring hard at my feet.

"Oh, you like my new boots?" I asked.

Chapman smiled. "The things you kids will wear."

"Heh-heh. Yeah, I guess I'm just a fashion victim."

I got out of there fast. By the time I made it to the girls' room my feet had returned to normal. I walked barefoot to the gym and got my gym shoes.

I was shaking more than I had from falling into the crocodiles the day before.

After all, a crocodile can only kill you. Chapman is a Yeerk. And they can do things that make plain old death seem easy.

CHAPTER 13

I meant to ask Ax about my little problem. I had promised Cassie I would. But right after school we had the mission. And if I'd brought it up then, everyone would have made me stay home.

Maybe that would have been the smart thing to do.

But it seemed to me that the sudden, surprise morphing had occurred just twice. The first time it had been a total catastrophe. But the second time only my feet had morphed.

Obviously, whatever was the matter with me, I was getting better. Probably it would never even happen again.

Probably.

I called my dad on his cell phone when I got out of school. "Daddy? Are you in a meeting or anything?"

"No, honey, I'm outside the courthouse waiting for this man I'm supposed to be interviewing. What's up? Are you okay?"

"Yeah, I haven't fallen into anything or had any buildings collapse on me. So far. I just wanted to let you know I'll be hanging with Cassie. We'll probably go to the mall or the library or something."

"Okay. Well, be sure to be back at the hotel by six, okay? I want to have dinner with you. Take a cab. Do you have enough money?"

"Yes. I'll see you for dinner."

Then I called my mom at work, got her voice mail, and left the same basic message.

It was sad how easy lying had become for me. I guess a lot of kids lie occasionally to their parents. But I have to do it way too much. Someday I'll be able to tell everyone the whole truth. That will be a relief.

Anyway, we were all supposed to meet up in the air above the beach. That was the plan. All of us except Ax and Tobias had the perfect morphs for the occasion. But it was one I hadn't used in a long time.

The tricky part was finding a safe place to morph. I headed for the stand of trees beyond the athletic field. Unfortunately, kids went there sometimes, and I couldn't risk being seen.

Fortunately, Tobias arrived to help.

<Hey, Rachel. If you can hear me, scratch your head.>

I scratched my head and casually looked up to the sky. I spotted the red-tailed hawk outlined against a fluffy white cloud.

<There are three people in the stand of woods, but they're walking away. They'll be gone by the time you get there.>

I couldn't answer because you can only make thought-speak when you're in a morph. But I trusted Tobias totally. Hawk eyes are about ten times better than human eyes. Tobias could have told me how many mice and rats and skunks and toads and squirrels were in that stand of woods. Let alone how many big, noisy, clunky humans were there.

I walked quickly into the trees. There was a ton of trash: soda cans and chip wrappers and McDonald's bags. I laughed, because for the morph I was going into, this was like the perfect world.

<You're still clear,> Tobias called down. <Four guys heading toward you from the school, but you'll be out of there before they arrive.>

I nodded. Then I focused on the morph. And I tried *not* to focus on the fact that morphing had gotten very weird since the day before. Like it was normal the rest of the time.

I began to shrink very quickly. Pine needles and dead leaves and beer cans and assorted trash all came rushing up.

Shrinking is weird because it's so much like falling. You don't think, *Oh, I'm getting small.* You think, *Oh, I'm falling!*

You fall and fall and fall, but somehow you never actually land. It's just that a can that started off seeming to be as big as your foot becomes as big as half your body. And a McDonald's bag that you could have stepped on is now so large you could crawl inside it. Leaves smaller than your hand are now as big as those little bathroom rugs.

As I shrank, I could see my flesh turning white. White as snow. White as paper. And then, when I was a creepy, shrinking ghost, the feather patterns begin to appear. They were tiny, close, delicate feathers. Much smaller than the owl or eagle morphs I used.

My teeth melded together and began to force themselves outward, forming a single hornlike protrusion. It pushed out and split open horizontally, creating a hooked beak.

I spread my arms wide and saw that they were already wings. Not the broad, powerful wings of

71

an eagle. Shorter, sharper, narrower, more acrobatic wings.

I had become the bird that is never endangered. The bird that lives on all seven of the seven continents. The bird that seems to thrive in every environment.

I was the mighty seagull.

Eater of fish, french fries, melted candy, eggs, Burger King Whoppers, popcorn, beef jerky, pickle slices, maraschino cherries, cheese puffs, burritos, and basically any other food that has ever been invented.

King of scavengers! Lord of the trash!

I flapped my wings and took to the sky. I flapped hard and rose to treetop level. And below me, the beauty of the world was revealed to my alert, seagull vision.

Food was everywhere! Everywhere humans threw garbage was a restaurant to me. The Dumpster behind the school! The parking lot of the convenience store! I saw it all. I spotted every blowing candy wrapper. I noted every single bit of roadkill.

Other birds had to kill to eat. Other birds had narrow, cramped environmental niches with just one or two kinds of acceptable food. Not me. I could live on junk food and garbage.

And that's why the skies were filled with my brothers and sisters. I saw them everywhere, always near the ground, always on the lookout for the next bread crumb.

Above me I spotted a dangerous form . . . the dark silhouette of a bird of prey. But I wasn't too worried. He was high up, and I was fast and very agile.

I flapped hard and flew fast, zooming like a wobbly, erratic rocket above the treetops, over the roofs, flitting through telephone wires, skimming easily over lawns and yards and gardens.

<Enjoying yourself, Rachel?>

What the . . . ?

<Hello. Hello in there, Rachel. You're not falling into the morph, are you?>

It took a few seconds for me to track. The voice in my head was Tobias. Tobias was a human. So was I.

Oh. Hello. Wake up, Rachel.

<Sorry, Tobias. I was getting kind of caught up in the seagull's head there for a minute. I wasn't prepared. I've done the morph before, so I wasn't on guard.>

It was embarrassing, actually. When you first do a morph it's very hard to control the mind of the animal. I mean, when I'd morphed the crocodile, even though I was totally prepared, I'd been ready to chomp that kid.

But I'd done the seagull before. I shouldn't have had any difficulty with it.

73

<You okay, Rachel?> Tobias asked.

<Yeah. Yeah. I'm fine, all right? I just wish everyone would stop asking me how I am. I'm *fine.*>

This wasn't related to the problem with un-controlled morphing. This was just a minor thing. A minor loss of concentration.

Nothing to worry about. That's what I told my-self.

<You know your way to the beach from here?>

<Of course I know the way to the beach,> I said, still mad for no good reason.

<Ooookay. See you there.>

Tobias peeled off and I flew on. One thing the seagull knew was how to find the beach.

But I was not a happy little seagull.

Something was wrong with me, and it wasn't going away.

CHAPTER 14

We met high above the beach. Four seagulls, looking totally normal among the hundreds of other seagulls. And higher up, floating on the thermals, a red-tailed hawk and a harrier.

The harrier was Ax. He'd never acquired a seagull. The harrier morph was a type of hawk, about the same size as Tobias.

<Okay, is everyone up for this?> Jake asked.

He was one of the wheeling, screaming seagulls around me, but I couldn't be sure which one.

<Let's do it!> I said. That's what I almost always say at the start of a mission. Everyone expected me to say it.

The truth was, I felt nervous and worried and totally unsure of myself. But people expected me to be all gung ho. If I hadn't been, they'd have known something was very wrong with me.

<What a shock,> Marco said sarcastically. <Mighty Xena is ready to go. Someone alert the media! It's a major story!>

<Oh, shut up, Marco,> I said.

<Okay, we fly out, find this yacht, then figure out how to proceed from there,> Jake said. <Right?>

<If we can find the yacht at all,> Marco said.

<Not a problem. It's out there, maybe three miles, heading southeast. There are three people on deck. I can't see their faces.> Tobias laughed. <Hawk vision, boys and girls. You seagulls stick to Dumpster-diving. I'll take care of long-range spying.>

<You sure it's the right boat?> Jake asked.

<The *Daybreeze*, right?>

<There is no way you can read the name on a boat that's three miles out,> Marco said. <I've been an osprey, remember? Your eyes are good, but you're not Superman.>

<Busted,> Tobias said. <Okay, I can't read the whole name on the boat. But I can see the *D*. And I took a good guess. I'm betting that's our wussy-boy actor.>

<Good enough,> I said. <Let's take a closer look.> It was all the usual banter before we go on a mission. It felt good to be doing something. Ac-

tion was better than sitting around waiting to see if I was going to morph out of control.

And I was still looking forward to actually seeing Jeremy Jason McCole. There was still the possibility we could rescue him or something.

Tobias said, <I better bail out on you guys. I'm not good over water. No thermals. Ax's harrier will be weak, too, but he can always morph to something else and swim back. I can't.>

We said good-bye to Tobias. I know he hates not being able to go with us on every mission. He feels like he's not doing enough, I guess. Which is stupid because really, no one does more for the cause than Tobias.

And none of us has paid a higher price in this war with the Yeerks than Tobias has.

We flapped away, slowly emerging from the dogfight of seagulls in the sky. We crossed the line from sand to surf. And then we kept going, out over green water and on to the deeper blue.

There was a breeze blowing against us and it was a struggle to make headway. But this was what seagulls were built to do. The seagull brain knew how to exploit every lull in the breeze. And the body was almost tireless.

Ax's harrier, on the other hand, was having a harder time. Hawks are made for soaring, or swooping down on their prey. They are great at riding the thermals, the big, billowy updrafts of warm air. But they aren't distance flyers. They can't just flap their wings endlessly.

But he still had better long-range vision than we did.

<I see the boat clearly now,> Ax announced. He didn't complain, but he sounded tired. <I can read the name *Daybreeze* very clearly. There are now four humans on the deck. Two older males. One female of medium age. One juvenile male.>

<Is it Jeremy Jason?> Cassie asked excitedly.

<Has to be,> I said.

<Does he have brownish-blond hair and really big blue eyes?>

<And full lips?> I added. <Like Brad Pitt lips?>

<Gag! Barf!> Marco, of course.

<The hair and eyes are correct,> Ax said. <I can't evaluate the lips, though. How large would lips have to be in order to be Brad Pitt lips?>

<In that Montana movie Brad Pitt's lips filled the entire screen,> Marco said. <In fact, I heard some people were crushed to death by Brad Pitt's lips.>

<Bet they're fake,> Jake muttered. <You know how they inject, like, butt fat into lips to make them all puffy?>

<It's so sad to hear so much jealousy, don't you agree, Cassie?>

<It is sad, Rachel. Terribly sad.>

<This is the worst mission we've ever been on,> Marco said. <I mean, I've been scared before. Hey, I've been horrified, screaming, wanting-to-wet-myself terrified before. I'm used to that. But this is the first time I've wanted to just throw up. Rachel, I didn't think you were even capable of normal human affection, let alone pathetic hero worship.>

<Say it, brother!> Jake agreed. I think he was kidding. But I couldn't be sure.

<And Cassie!> Marco went on. <I thought you only cared about animals. Animals like skunks and snakes . . . and Jake. Hee-hee!>

<Okay, let's get back to business now,> Jake said quickly.

Jake gets embarrassed any time anyone mentions his feelings for Cassie. And we were practically caught up to the yacht.

<Ax, buddy, I think you need to peel off. Change morphs and stay close by in the water.>

<Yes, Prince Jake.>

<Don't call me prince.>

<Yes, Prince Jake.>

<Marco and I will go in close, land on the boat like any ordinary seagulls, see what we overhear,> Jake went on. <Rachel and Cassie, you can be backup. Stay —>

<Yeah, *right*,> I jeered. <You and Marco go. Me and Cassie stay away. Yeah, that's really going to happen. Come on, Cassie, we're going in.>

I flapped hard to pull away from Jake and Marco. Ax gratefully peeled off, soaring back and away on the breeze.

The yacht was very large. I don't know how big, but it was big enough that the four people lounging on the aft deck could have played a game of volleyball if they'd wanted to. I mean, this was not some little motorboat.

Cassie and I moved behind the boat. Below us, propellers were churning the sea turquoise and white. Just ahead, we could clearly see the four people.

One was the movie producer wearing shorts and an open shirt. I'd seen him on CNN.

One was a man who stood with his back to us.

The third person was a woman in a bikini. She was young and pretty.

And the fourth person . . . yes! There was no mistaking that hair. That face. Those lips.

<It's him!> Cassie said.

<Oh, yes,> I agreed.

Jeremy Jason McCole. Star of *Power House*. At least he was the star if you forgot about that comedian guy who played his father.

Jeremy Jason McCole, who had appeared in

basically every fanzine published in the last five years. Most of which either Cassie or I had read.

<His favorite color is crimson,> Cassie said. <It's so cool. He didn't just say "red." He said "crimson.">

<He was born in Altoona, Pennsylvania.>

<He has two sisters. Their names are Jessica and Madison.>

<Nice chest.>

<Nice legs.>

<Let's get closer,> I said.

We flapped a little and found ourselves in a sweet pocket of air. The boat created its own breeze, which sort of carried us along. We barely had to flap our wings. We could just hang in the air over the back end of the boat. We hung there, enjoying the view from ten feet above Jeremy Jason McCole. We listened to the conversation between the actor, the producer, and the two other people.

And it was then that I fell out of love with the extremely cute Jeremy Jason McCole.

CHAPTER 15

The wind carried some of what they said away. The noise of the churning water and the big engines wiped some of it out. But we heard enough, Cassie and I. Too much.

". . . don't want to be on the losing side of this, Jeremy," the producer was saying. "Face it, your TV career is over."

"It's not over as long as . . . million teen-age . . . in love with me," Jeremy said.

"All I'm saying is, big changes are coming. Big changes like . . . has ever seen before, okay? Now, my company is part of the new order. You do business . . . parts in movies. Serious parts. Let you move beyond teenage roles."

Jeremy Jason laughed. "That'd be nice. I'm

about sick to death of dopey . . . sending me love letters and mobbing me for autographs. See, that's part of the problem I have with your offer. You'll have me still. . . . I'm sick of . . . be Mr. Goody Good all the time."

Then the other man, the one who had been standing with his back to us, stepped forward. He barely flicked a finger and the producer backed away. The woman in the bikini narrowed her eyes and seemed to shrink down in her chair.

"Let's stop wasting time," the man said. "We've been talking . . . yesterday . . . better things to do. I can give you . . . thing you want. *Everything*. Money . . . power. But first, you have to agree to my. . . . They are . . . simple. You become one of us. And then, you take on this . . . representing The Sharing. In exchange . . . anything and everything your heart desires."

Jeremy Jason sat silently while the man spoke. The man scared him. That was obvious. When Jeremy Jason did speak, it was in a low, strained voice. "And if I say no?"

"You won't say no," the man said. He turned then, and I saw his face. I saw an icy smile, and cold, dead eyes.

I had seen him before, just briefly. But once was enough.

<Visser Three!> Cassie hissed.

The Visser was in his human morph. But it

was him. And having recognized him, it was as if the sun was gone from the sky. I felt darkness reaching out from him. Darkness that clutched at my heart.

Visser Three, leader of the Yeerk invasion of Earth. The only Yeerk ever to take control of an Andalite body. The only Yeerk to possess the Andalite morphing power.

Visser Three, the evil creature who had murdered Ax's brother Elfangor while we sat terrified, helpless.

He smiled his icy, fake-human smile for Jeremy Jason. "You're an ambitious. . . . You want. . . . So much more than you will ever get without my help."

Suddenly Jeremy Jason laughed. "I guess you see through me." He stood up to face the frightening man. "I let you perform this procedure . . . make me a major movie star. Deal?"

The cold smile reappeared. "Deal."

<He can't possibly know what this means!> Cassie cried. <They've tricked him.>

<Yeah. They have. But you know what? He wouldn't be falling for it unless he was a creep.>

<I don't care,> Cassie said. <We can't let them make Jeremy Jason a Controller!>

<No, we'll have to try and save him,> I agreed. <But now I wonder if he's worth it.> I felt sick inside. I know it's dumb to have a crush on

some actor you only know from TV. But it's a nice, normal kind of dumb. And I didn't have much normal anything in my life.

<Let's get back with Jake and Marco,> I said. <Man. They are so going to rag on us over this. Jeremy Jason ready to become a voluntary Controller. It's disgusting.>

I banked sharply away, caught the headwind again, and realized that I was getting lower. Lower very quickly. I flapped harder.

<Rachel! What are you doing?> Cassie yelled.

<I don't know! I can't seem to fly!>

<Oh, no! You're morphing, Rachel! Stop!>

My wings were beating the air, but I just kept falling. And then I saw the reason. It was right in front of my face.

Literally!

Where my small, hooked seagull beak should have been, something long and gray was growing.

<I'm growing a trunk!> I cried.

From their positions a hundred yards behind the boat, Marco and Jake spotted the disaster-in-the-making.

<Rachel! What are you doing?> Jake yelled.

<I can't stop! I can't stop! I'm morphing!>

The trunk was now half-a-foot long and my wings were not even close to powerful enough. I fell. I hit the water with a splash.

But not before I caught a glimpse of Visser

Three. He was standing at the back rail of the boat. He was staring right at me with dead, evil eyes.

I hit the water and kept going. The elephant morph seemed to be speeding up. I was morphing at a speed unlike anything I'd ever done before.

Down I sank. Down and down as bubbles spiraled up away from me. My huge leathery ears were growing from my head. I felt my bones grinding as they swiftly became massive and thick and long.

I tried to tread water, but I had legs like tree trunks!

The sparkling surface of the water above me already looked as far away as the surface of the moon. I was drowning.

<Rachel! Morph out!> Cassie screamed.

<Ax!> Jake yelled. <If you can hear me, find Rachel. Stay with her!>

But I knew the others couldn't reach me in time. I was falling and falling, down and down through the water. My trunk could not reach air, although I stretched it high over my head.

I was drowning in an elephant's body. And all I could do was wonder why.

CHAPTER 16

I fell down through the water, down toward the invisible ocean floor a mile below me.

I tried to focus. To find a way to demorph. But I couldn't. My mind was slipping away.

I was about fifty feet under when it occurred to me to see whether the elephant could swim. I mean, it seemed stupid. Of course elephants can't swim. But what did I have to lose?

I started running in water with my big telephone pole legs and to my utter amazement it turned out the elephant *could* swim. But too late to do me much good. I was too far down. I'd never reach air in time.

I saw a flash of gray, a deadly shape in the water beside me. I heard, like it was from far off, a thought-speak voice saying, <I see her, Prince Jake!>

Somehow it almost made me laugh. It was a talking shark. Why was a shark talking?

Then . . . panic!

I began thrashing wildly. I churned the water, motoring my big legs, futilely trying to rise faster. I flung my trunk this way and that. But panic was no better than peaceful surrender. I was rising, but it was too little, too late.

And yet . . .

<She's demorphing!> the talking shark said. <No . . . wait. Prince Jake, she is not demorphing. I mean, not back to human. She is going straight to some other morph!>

<That's impossible!>

<I know. But that's what is happening!>

<I'm going after her,> Cassie yelled. <I'll dive underwater, out of sight. I'll morph to human, then try to morph to dolphin before I run out of air. Maybe I can help her.>

<Do it,> Jake snapped. <Marco, stay up top. I'm going down with Cassie.>

<She is getting smaller at an impressive speed,> Ax, the talking shark, said.

The talking shark was right. I was shrinking. Shrinking at a shocking speed. Shrinking so fast

I created a little whirlpool where my massive elephant bulk was disappearing.

<Jake! Look!> Marco yelled. <That man on the boat! He's morphing. I swear, he's turning into an Andalite! Oh, man. Him!>

<Yes, it's Visser Three,> Cassie said. <Forget him. We have to save Rachel!>

Morphing, morphing, morphing. *Everyone is morphing,* I thought in my giddy, nearly unconscious mind.

I decided it would make a good song. <Oh what fun it is to morph, to morph and morph today. Hey!>

<Is she singing "Jingle Bells"?> Marco demanded.

<Ax, I'm in dolphin morph now, but I can't see Rachel. Where are you two?> Cassie cried. <I should be able to see an elephant and a shark!>

<Rachel is no longer an elephant. In fact, I can't see her at all. She's too small.>

<What?> Jake asked.

<We're almost there! Ax, you have to find her!>

I rose slowly from the brink of unconsciousness. Slowly, the gears in my brain started to grind forward. I was underwater. I was sure of that. But I was no longer the elephant.

I could breathe! And I was no longer sinking.

At least, it didn't feel like I was. But I couldn't see to be sure. I was blind.

Don't panic, Rachel, I ordered myself. But that was easier said than done. I was blind!

<I can't find her,> Ax yelled in frustration. <These shark eyes are too weak. She was too small. I think she was morphing an insect.>

Insect?

Slowly, reluctantly, I took stock. I had legs. I could move them, feel them. Four legs. No, six! Yes, I had become an insect. I had feelers. I waved them around and tasted the air. Nothing. Just my own smell.

And what brain was in with my own? None. No awareness. No thought. It was the body of a mindless machine. There were two possibilities: termite . . . or *ant*!

<Ax? Cassie? I think . . . I think I went into ant morph!> I cried. <Nobody swallow anything. It could be me.>

<Are you okay?> Cassie asked.

<You mean aside from the fact that I'm in ant morph, trapped inside an air bubble in the middle of the ocean?> I said, more sarcastically than I should have. <Yeah, aside from all that, I'm great.>

<Uh-oh,> Marco said.

<Uh-oh *what*?> Jake snapped.

<Uh-oh, Visser Three is going from Andalite form to something else.>

<What is it? What's he morphing?>

<I don't know what it is. But it's big and it looks like it could swim.>

<Oh, man! Can anything else go wrong?!> Jake yelled in frustration. <Rachel, can you demorph? Can you get human? Or dolphin? Or *something* useful?>

<I don't know.> I tried to calm my panicky, jumbled mind. I tried to focus on morphing. On getting human again.

Come on, Rachel, you can do this, I told myself. But I had the feeling I was lying.

And yet I could feel myself growing once more. I felt myself press against the rubbery walls of the air bubble.

<I think I see her!> Cassie said. <No, wait. Just seaweed. No, wait again. I *do* see her. She's green, maybe half an inch long but growing fast.>

<Rachel, what are you morphing?> Jake asked.

<Why don't you tell me? Because, guess what? I DON'T KNOW!>

<Stay cool, Rachel,> Jake advised.

<Cool? *Cool?* Hey, sorry if I sound tense, but I keep turning into things I don't want to turn into.>

91

<It's the crocodile!> Cassie said. <Jake, over here. This way.>

Suddenly, I could see again. Eyes appeared just in time for me to see sticklike ant legs morphing into stubby, green-scaled crocodile legs.

I was growing at incredible speed. I could feel the water sliding over and around me as I occupied more and more space. But at least I could see again. And I wasn't drowning. The crocodile has the ability to hold its breath for a very long time.

Above me I could see the bright sheet that was the divider between water and air. And in the water around me hovered two big, gray bottlenose dolphins, both grinning their eternal dolphin grins. Cassie and Jake.

Moving swiftly past, just a hundred feet off, was a menacing-looking tiger shark. Ax. I hoped.

I looked at Jake. Or maybe it was Cassie. <I guess maybe I should have mentioned I was having this little problem with morphing, huh?>

<No, it's much better to find out this way, Rachel. You know — when you could get us all killed,> Jake said.

It's not like Jake to be sarcastic.

<Oh, man,> Marco said. He was still in seagull morph. <I don't know what Visser Three is now, but he's getting ready to dive in the

water. And you don't want to be there when he does.>

<Let's get out of here while we can,> Jake said. <Rachel, if you feel any more morphing happening, tell us, all right? If you don't mind.>

<Yell at me later, okay? Let's get some distance.>

I turned my long body easily and began swimming, using my big crocodile tail.

Cassie and Jake and Ax all turned on the speed and in ten seconds they were far out ahead of me. I saw Jake stop and look back.

<Alligators aren't exactly fast swimmers, are they?>

<Crocodiles,> I corrected him. <And no. I guess not.>

Then we heard . . .

PUH-WHUMPF!

It was a sound like a depth charge. Like something very large had just cannonballed into the water.

<Here he comes,> Marco announced grimly. <Look out for those spears. They look nasty.>

<The what?> I asked. <The *spears*? What spears?>

<The thing Visser Three morphed into. I can't be sure, but I think maybe it shoots spears out of its mouth.>

<Ah!> Ax said, speaking up. <I bet it's a Lebtin javelin fish! I've always wanted to see one of those. I mean . . . you know . . . in a zoo or something.>

<Well, we can't outrun it with Rachel in alligator morph,> Jake said.

<Crocodile,> Cassie said. <Not alligator.>

<You guys get out of here. I'll take care of Visser Three,> I said, sounding much braver than I felt. <It's my fault we're in this mess.>

<Yeah, right, Rachel,> Jake said.

Then he began rapid-fire orders. <Spread out. Thirty feet apart. Keep moving so he doesn't get an easy target. Marco? We could use your help down here. And for future reference, I don't give a rat's butt if it's a crocodile or an alligator, so long as it can fight.>

CHAPTER 17

I drifted up to the surface, showing just my nostrils and my eyes above water. I breathed out and refilled my lungs with fresh air.

The dolphins did the same, blowing out through the holes in the backs of their heads and sucking in fresh air.

In the few seconds before I dived again, I saw Jeremy Jason standing on the back of the boat. He had a huge, fierce grin on his face. He was pointing and laughing like a fan at a boxing match.

Something he yelled drifted to me on the breeze.

"Is he awesome, or what?!"

He was referring to Visser Three. He had just watched the Visser shed his human form, meld into his stolen Andalite body, then morph into a fearsome beast from some far-distant planet. And his reaction to it all was admiration.

I felt cold fury. What kind of a human being would sell out his own species?

Enjoy the show while you can, I sneered silently. *It may not end the way you expect.*

I sank back beneath the choppy waves, down and down. And then I saw it. *Him.* Visser Three.

It was a bizarre morph. Like nothing on Earth, that's for sure. It looked like a vast, bright yellow stingray. Like a living pancake, flat and oblong. It sort of flew through the water by slowly flapping its sides. There were two stalk-mounted eyes on top, and two long, trailing antennae below.

All along its back it had spears. They were lined up flat. You know how a fighter jet has missiles tucked up under the wings? That's how it held the spears, only they were on top. But all neatly in a row, facing forward.

The spears — there must have been twenty of them — were each as long as a broom handle and just about as thick. They had irregular striping, yellow and green and bits of blue. It was probably camouflage back on the home planet of the Lebtin javelin fish. But here, in Earth's oceans, it seemed gaudy and too bright.

It flew through the water. Faster than my crocodile could ever have moved. But faster, too, than the dolphins or the shark.

<Fast,> Jake said.

<Yep,> I agreed.

<Probably not all that agile, though,> he suggested.

<No. It will be slow in a turn.>

<I've changed my mind,> Ax said. <I do not think I want to see a Lebtin javelin fish.>

I glanced left. Ax was holding position there. Beyond him was Jake. Cassie was on my right. The javelin fish was now just a hundred feet away. I could only pray I wouldn't suddenly start morphing again.

Then . . .

The javelin fish — Visser Three — began to swell up. It seemed to inflate like a balloon. It slowed . . . slowed . . .

SHOOOOOOP!

A spear fired from the javelin fish's mouth! Like a rocket, it lanced through the water. I didn't have time to even think about dodging it.

<AHHHHHHH!>

The spear went through my tail, near the base. Pain shot up my spine. Blood billowed into the water around me. *My* blood!

I looked down. The spear was still there, piercing my scales. All I could do was stare at it.

It seemed ridiculous. It was just stuck right through me!

<Rachel!>

<Hah-HAH!> Visser Three exulted. <It works! I just acquired this morph, and look how well it performs!>

I looked at Visser Three. One of the spears stored on his back rolled neatly into a flap. Then he began to swell again, ready to fire another spear.

<Look out! Move! Move!> Jake howled in our heads.

But I couldn't move. My tail was paralyzed. I wanted to charge the alien creature, but I could barely move at all.

SHOOOOOOP!

The second spear flew straight for Cassie. But her dolphin was too fast. She kicked hard and the spear missed by millimeters.

No, she had been hit! I could see the cut across her back where the spear had opened the flesh.

<I'm okay, I'm okay!> she cried.

She'd been lucky. A split-second slower and she would have been impaled.

The javelin fish was still rushing at us. I rolled onto my back, pale belly up. <Jake! Back off. Get out of here. It's too fast! You have to split up and hope you lose him!>

<I'm not leaving you!>

<You have to. I'll play dead. And if he comes close enough . . .>

He hesitated, but only for a second longer. <Split up! Run for it!>

<I'm not leaving Rachel!> Cassie cried.

<Cassie, you have to,> I said. <Now! Get out of here or we'll all be dead!>

Visser Three flew toward us, gliding swiftly through the water. I saw a new spear roll into the flap. He began to swell, sucking in the water he used to propel the spear.

<He's getting ready again. You guys, GET OUT OF HERE!>

Cassie and Jake and Ax all wheeled sharply away, each heading off in a different direction.

SHOOOOOOP!

The spear raced after Ax! He was a hundred feet away and moving at full shark speed. But the spear gained swiftly.

<Now, Ax! Now!> I yelled.

He swerved right, and the spear blew past.

<Thank you, Rachel,> Ax said.

The Visser hesitated. <Ah, splitting up, eh? Well, that will only affect the order in which I kill each of you. What have I heard the human children say? Ah yes, eeny, meeny, miney, moo.>

I almost said, "It's *moe*, you jerk. Moe, not *moo*."

But I had slightly more sense than that. I just lay there, hanging in the water, belly-up, looking dead and trying not to feel the pain from the spear in my tail.

Go after Cassie, I begged silently. *Go for Cassie, you disgusting creature.*

If the Visser went after Ax, he would pass too far from me to reach. The same if he chased Jake. Only Cassie would bring him near me.

Visser Three flapped his water wings.

I grinned a crocodile grin.

He came closer, closer, then he slowed and began to swell. Larger and larger he grew, like an overfilled balloon. And closer and closer he came.

Ten feet . . . five . . . two . . . twelve inches . . .

Close enough.

I jerked every muscle in my powerful crocodile body. My head thrust forward. My jaws opened wide.

And I bit down.

I definitely bit down.

Did you know a crocodile has the most powerful jaws in the animal kingdom? Did you know they can practically crush rocks with their jaws?

I clamped that long, toothy crocodile jaw down on the left wing of the Visser's javelin fish. And then . . .

POOOOMPFF!

SPWOOOOSH!

It was like biting into a water balloon. The inflated javelin fish exploded. All the water it had sucked in to fire its next spear went blasting out through the hole I made.

And that Lebtin javelin fish learned a whole new way to fly. It squirted wildly through the water, blasted up through the surface, arced through the air like a sick dolphin, and landed far away with a loud, satisfying splash.

And the whole time, we heard Visser Three's thought-speak voice crying, <Ahhhhhhhhhhh!>

I relaxed a little then, although relaxing just made me notice the pain in my tail. A dolphin came nosing up to me.

<Hey, it's me, Marco. I'm here to save the day!>

I actually laughed. <Just in time, Marco. Just in time.>

CHAPTER 18

<Allergy,> Ax said. <You acquired some animal you're allergic to. It happens sometimes.>

"This out-of-control morphing is an allergy? I have an allergy? To what?"

"What was the last animal you acquired?" Cassie asked. Then she answered her own question. "The crocodile. You must be allergic to crocodiles."

We were in the safety of the woods out beyond Cassie's farm. It was a little area we went to fairly often for privacy. Ax needed to morph back to his own body. And Tobias . . . well, Tobias needed to hunt dinner before it got dark.

As we all talked, Tobias waited in an overhead

branch. We were on the edge of a small, grassy meadow. A meadow full of mice.

Tobias kept his laser vision focused on the tall grass of the meadow. The others were all glaring at me. Except Cassie, of course, who was just shaking her head. She felt she'd made a mistake letting me keep my secret.

"You're saying because I acquired that crocodile I lost control of my morphing powers?"

<Not *all* control. Just some. It's . . . it's like when you humans suddenly make violent exhalations through your nostrils and shout, "Achoo!">

"Sneezing. You're saying I've been sneezing."

<Hah!> Tobias said. He opened his wings and swooped out across the grass, just a few feet above the ground. He flared suddenly, raked his talons forward, and for a few seconds disappeared from sight.

"And another mouse bites the dust," Marco commented.

<Yes, Rachel,> Ax said. <You've been having an allergic reaction to the crocodile DNA.>

"So what do I do? Is there some medicine I can take or something?"

<No medicine. At least none that humans could create. But there is a process. Something that happens naturally in these cases. At least it happens to Andalites. It's called *hereth illint*.>

103

"That sounds poetic," Cassie said.

<A literal translation would be something like "burping DNA.">

"Now *that's* poetry," Marco said, laughing.

<Since we have no mouths we don't have phrases like "spitting out" or "vomiting up." *Hereth* is what we say instead.>

Even Jake smiled. "How does Rachel do it? This process?" he asked Ax.

<The offending DNA will eventually be expelled from your system. You can't control *when* it happens. You just have to be careful, especially since this crocodile is a dangerous creature.>

"Sounds easy enough," I said. "I'm always careful."

<It isn't easy. See, you basically have to morph the animal *while* you retain your own body. You have to create a whole, living animal out of the excess matter floating in Zero-space.>

I looked at Ax. "Excuse me?"

<Until the *hereth illint* begins, you can control some of the symptoms by remaining very calm and unemotional. The out-of-control morphing in the water happened when you were upset or emotional.>

I shrugged. "I was mad because that jerk Jeremy Jason McTraitor was betraying his fans. Not to mention his entire species, yeah."

<And you said a similar thing happened when

you were in Chapman's office, where you were afraid.>

I nodded. "Uh-huh. I mean, not like *afraid* afraid. Just sort of nervous afraid."

<And the first time? When you morphed inside your house? What emotion were you feeling then?>

"Nothing." I kept my face blank.

"What were you doing when it started?" Jake asked me.

"I don't remember," I lied.

Cassie cocked an eyebrow at me. "Rachel, you were pulling up pictures of Jeremy Jason off the Internet."

"So?" I demanded. "That's not something emotional!"

"It was l-o-o-o-v-e," Marco crowed, drawing the word out. "The deadly, dangerous emotion of puppy love. Rachel was overcome by attraction! By desire! By intense, uncontrollable *Tiger Beat* passion! And it —"

He was interrupted by the fact that I tried to grab him and choke him. But he dodged behind Ax.

"It turned her into a wild animal!" Marco yapped on. "Several wild animals, actually. She became the alligator of l-o-o-o-v-e!"

"It's crocodile," Jake said, smirking in a most un-Jakelike way.

105

And then, suddenly, I realized a feather pattern began to appear on my skin. Bald eagle feathers. I groaned.

<You see?> Ax said, noticing the beginning of the morph. <Passions and emotions set off the allergic reaction. You must try to eliminate the emotions.>

"How about if I just eliminate Marco?" I growled.

"It's so perfect," Marco said. "Mighty *Xena* has a weakness: human emotion. She's a victim of l-o-o-o-v-e."

Jake grabbed Marco's arm and squeezed tight. "Marco, if you make her mad, she'll morph. And if she starts morphing, she might end up in full grizzly bear. Do you really want Rachel mad at you and in grizzly bear morph?"

Marco hesitated. He glanced at me. He bit his lip. "I get your point, Jake. I think I'll just go watch Tobias eat his mouse."

I was halfway feathered by the time I was able to reverse the morph. It took that long to calm down.

"Ax, tell Rachel whatever you can about this *hereth* thing. Get her prepared. And Rachel, until you are better, keep a very low profile. As in don't go to school. And forget about this TV show you were going to do with Jeremy Jason. Visser Three knows we're on to Jeremy Jason. The Visser will make him a Controller immediately. Actor boy has seen too much. They're probably infesting him right now."

"But we still have to stop him! We can't have him speaking for The Sharing. We could grab him, keep him locked up somewhere for three days till the Yeerk in his head dies."

"I know we have to stop him, and we will. We'll just have to figure out some other way to get at him."

"He's probably going to start endorsing The Sharing on the *Barry and Cindy Sue Show*. Then he'll leave town," I argued. "It's our last chance. They'll be on guard now. They'll be watching for us. We'll *never* get near that stupid yacht again. That show may be our last shot at him!"

Jake nodded. "Could be. Could be we can't pull this off. Could be we'll have to forget about it." The good-humored smile evaporated. He gave me a cold look. "Maybe you should have thought about all that, Rachel. You're the one who blew the mission today. You're the one who let Visser Three know we were on to Jeremy Jason. Next time maybe you'll let the rest of us know when you're not in shape to handle a mission."

I would have argued . . . if I could have. But everything he was saying was true.

I glanced at Cassie. She was looking down at the ground, embarrassed. Ax made a point of aiming all four of his eyes away, like he was watching something fascinating far off in the distance.

I couldn't see Tobias. He was still out in the tall grass. But he must have overheard because he whispered to me, <Hey, don't worry about it, Rachel. It's okay.>

"No. It's not," I whispered.

CHAPTER 19

Okay, yes, I had screwed up. But I was determined to fix the problem.

So I basically lied.

The next day I told Jake and Cassie that it had happened. The *hereth illint*. I told them it had happened in great detail. I went on and on about how weird it was. I was very convincing. And they fell for it.

Of course, if I'd tried to fool Ax it wouldn't have worked. Because see, I didn't really know what was going to happen during this DNA burping. None of us had really understood Ax when he'd explained it. Once he starts in about Zerospace, we all just kind of glaze over.

But if I *had* tried to trick Ax, he would have

asked the one question neither Jake nor Cassie thought to ask: What did you do with the extra crocodile?

Anyway, when I saw Jake the next day in school and told him it was all over, he believed me. Even Cassie believed me because I told her in a hurried whisper as we changed classes. I think if I'd had to look her right in the face, she would have known I was lying.

I had no choice. I *had* to make it to the *Barry and Cindy Sue Show*. One way or another, whatever it took, we had to stop Jeremy Jason from endorsing The Sharing on that show.

See, I knew I was okay. Because all I had to do was to control my emotions. Just stay unemotional, and I wouldn't go into uncontrolled morphs. And I'm good at handling emotion.

Except anger, maybe. I have a small problem with anger.

But who was going to make me mad on a stupid TV show? It would be fine. Fine.

Uh-huh.

After school I took a taxi again to my dad's hotel. I had the taxi pass by my house. Work crews were already there, ripping out the shattered remains of our kitchen and my bedroom. They had one of those super-sized Dumpsters out front, full of plasterboard and two-by-fours.

"Did you hear what happened to that place?"

the taxi driver asked me. "House just fell apart. I tell you, the way they build things nowadays."

To my surprise my dad was actually at the hotel, waiting for me.

"About time!" he said, a little frantically as soon as I walked in the room. "The show goes live at five o'clock! It's almost three! Where have you been?"

"School."

"Oh. Yeah. School. Come on, come on. Fortunately, we can walk to the studio and avoid traffic. It's just down the street. Five minutes."

Choosing an outfit took very little time: I only had about three things salvaged from the wreck of my bedroom. I quickly called Cassie to tell her to hurry, too. She was supposed to meet me at the studio.

She wasn't home, which probably meant she was already waiting for me. That was the plan. Cassie would be with me. The others would try to get into the studio in innocent-looking morphs. But we knew the Yeerks would be watching the place. They'd probably have some of their people in the audience. And for all any of us knew, Barry or Cindy Sue themselves might be Controllers.

"Are you nervous?" my dad asked as we hustled rapidly down the street.

"Not really," I said.

"Nationwide, live TV broadcast? Millions of

people watching? Coast-to-coast? And you're not nervous?"

"Now I am," I muttered. I suppressed the nervousness. I couldn't afford to feel anything. I just had to get through this without feeling any extreme emotion. I could do that.

We blew past the receptionist at the studio, my dad in the lead, looking like Mr. Big Time, and me double-stepping to keep up. Cassie was waiting in the lobby and got swept up with us.

"How you doing?" she asked me.

I shrugged. "Great."

"Really?"

"Yep."

"Nervous?"

"No."

"Excited?"

"No."

"Scared."

"Definitely not."

She leaned close and whispered. "Do we have a plan? I mean, what exactly are we doing about Jeremy Jason?"

I shrugged. "We're stopping him."

"How?"

I grinned. "We're improvising."

"Uh-oh."

Suddenly, a llama came tearing past. Its

dainty hooves skittered crazily on the waxed linoleum. It turned a corner and was gone.

"What the . . ." my dad said.

"Cool," Cassie said. Her eyes lit up the way they do when she sees any animal. "It's a llama. They're really neat animals, you know. They —"

Suddenly two people dressed in khaki raced up and shoved past us. They turned the corner after the llama and were gone.

The three of us just stood there staring at each other. Then a third person, a woman with a clipboard, ran up breathlessly. "Did you see a llama?"

I pointed. "That way."

"Hey, what's the deal?" my dad asked.

The woman shook her head like the world was coming to an end. "Bart Jacobs's on the show with his animals. The llama made a run for it. Smart animal."

"Bart Jacobs?" The name sounded familiar. "Isn't he that guy who takes animals on the talk shows?"

Cassie made a disapproving look. "That's him, all right. I hate seeing wild animals dragged into studios and treated like —"

"Well. If there are no more wild animals," my dad interrupted, "we have to keep moving." He started off again and we fell into step behind him. He swept us in his wake toward the makeup room. The door was open. A woman with weird hair and black lipstick looked at my dad and gave a little leer. Then she looked at me and Cassie, like she was trying to figure out what to do with our faces.

"She's the one," my father said, pointing at me. "Rachel, meet Tai. Tai, my daughter Rachel. She's on the show."

"The skin is beautiful," Tai said. "But I think we want more body in the hair." She grabbed a handful of my hair and sort of threw it disdainfully. "What do you use on your hair?"

I told her the brand. She sneered. My dad took off to schmooze with some people he knew. And Tai shoved me into a barbershop-style chair, whipped a sheet over me, and began doing things with brushes.

I hate being shoved around like that.

It really kind of made me mad.

"This hair! This hair!" Tai complained. Then she yanked. Way too hard.

I hate being yanked.

Suddenly, Tai backed away. "What is happening to your hair? It's . . . it's turning gray!"

I looked past her to the mirror. I saw two things. I saw Cassie's horrified expression. And I saw my hair turning gray. Gray and shaggy.

Like a wolf.

It was happening! I'd gotten mad at Tai and I was morphing. Into a wolf! I shot a desperate glance at Cassie. Cassie acted instantly. "Look!" she cried. "Out in the hallway! It's . . . um . . . it's Kevin Costner! And Tom Cruise, too!"

Tai screamed, "Where? Where?" dropped her brush and ran for the door.

I focused. *Calm . . . calm . . . no emotion . . .*

But Cassie wasn't helping. At all. "You lied! To *me*! Again! You didn't do that *hereth illint* thing at all! You're still allergic!"

"I'm trying to be calm, Cassie," I warned. "I'm trying to demorph."

"You can't do this stupid show while you're still this way!"

"I'm doing the show. It's the only way! I'm not letting this creep . . . now look! You're just making me upset!"

The gray fur was beginning to grow on the back of my arms and hands. I shut my eyes. *No anger. No anger. No anger.*

"I didn't see Kevin Costner out there," Tai said suspiciously when she returned.

"I was sure that was him," Cassie said. "Sorry."

"Now what was going on with your hair?" Tai asked, staring baffled at my now-normal head.

"Um . . . not enough conditioning?" I suggested.

And that's when I suffered my second emotional jolt. Because that's when the cutest boy on the planet walked into the makeup room.

"Jeremy Jason," I heard Cassie whisper in awestruck tones.

No emotion . . . no emotion . . . , I told myself.

But you have no idea just how massively cute he was up close like that. And then he smiled at Cassie, and gave her a little half-hug. Like he'd probably done with a million fans before.

I saw Cassie's knees buckle. She actually wobbled.

"Hi, I'm Jeremy Jason McCole," he said to me. "Are you on the show, too?"

"Yes," I said, trying to sound like a robot. "Yes, I am on the show, too."

I didn't get up from the makeup chair. And I didn't shake his hand. Because I have to tell you the truth: Even knowing what he was now, even knowing what kind of person he was, even knowing that inside his head there lived an evil gray Yeerk slug, if he'd hugged me like he had Cassie, I would have morphed.

I would have morphed big time.

CHAPTER 20

"Hey," Jeremy Jason said, giving me his famous squinty, skeptical look. "Don't I know you from somewhere?"

I shook my head. "No. Definitely not."

"Yeah, yeah. You're the girl who fell into the crocodile pit after that kid. You're on the show today, huh?"

"That's not all she did," Cassie rushed to say. "She also had her house fall in on her."

I sent Cassie a "What are you doing?" look. Like having a house fall on me would make Jeremy Jason think better of me? Like that would impress him?

Cassie made a helpless, confused, giddy look and shrugged. She kept staring at Jeremy Jason with this slightly weird grin. Of course, to be honest, I probably had the identical slightly weird grin.

Jeremy Jason flashed his smile. Then he said, "Look, Disaster Girl, or whatever you are, how about if you and your friend stumble on out of here? I need to get made up. And I don't need an audience."

That took care of the weird grins. Tai looked fiercely at me and jerked her head toward the door.

Outside in the hallway we found the llama. It was standing there, minding its own business.

"'Disaster Girl'?" I repeated. "Excuse me?"

"'Stumble on out of here'?" Cassie said.

We both looked at the llama.

"If you're waiting to get made up, you can forget it," I told the llama. "You're not a big enough star."

<Maybe not, but I will be someday,> the llama said.

"Yahah!" Cassie and I yelped. You'd think we, of all people, would be prepared for strange things like talking llamas. But it caught us totally by surprise.

"Marco?" I hissed.

<Who else would be this cute? Check out this fur. Check out this little llama smile on my little llama face.>

"What are you doing?"

<Jake's somewhere around here in cockroach morph. Ax is here in fly morph. I came that way, too. But then I saw this llama wandering around loose. So I thought, hey, why be a bug?>

"Where's the *real* llama?" Cassie whispered.

<Don't worry. I put him in an empty dressing room. By the way, I saw the schedule. Bart Jacobs and various animals of his, including yours truly, go on first, then the Wussy Wonder, and finally you, Rachel.>

Cassie cocked an eyebrow at me. I deliberately didn't look at her. I knew what she wanted me to do.

"Fine, *I'll* tell him," Cassie said. "Marco, Rachel may have slightly exaggerated when she said she was okay. You'd better warn Jake."

<She didn't burp the croc?>

"Nope."

"I'm fine as long as I don't get excited," I said defensively.

<You know, Rachel, *I'm* supposed to be the irresponsible one,> Marco said.

Cassie was biting her lip thoughtfully. "It's too late for Rachel just to cancel. But we need a backup, just in case. No matter what happens, we can't have people seeing Rachel morph."

<What can you do? If she morphs suddenly —>

119

"Well," Cassie interrupted, "the important thing is that there always be a Rachel. See? I can't believe what I'm even thinking, and it totally gives me the willies, but Rachel? I think we need a copy of you."

<Morph Rachel?> Marco trilled. <I'll do it! I'll do it!>

"When pigs fly," I said.

Marco shot a llama look to his left. <Uh-oh. Looks like I'm busted.>

The two khaki-clad trainers appeared at the end of the hallway. They crept up slowly. Marco waited patiently till they caught him, slipped a rope around his neck, and led him away.

<See you guys later,> Marco called back. <Break a leg. Not literally. That's just what we show biz people say to mean "good luck." I'm going to be on tee-vee-ee. I'm going to be on tee-vee-ee.>

Cassie laid her hand on my arm.

"What are you doing?" I asked.

"Don't worry, I'll never use your morph for anything bad," Cassie said solemnly. And then I started getting dreamy and drifty as she acquired my DNA.

"Don't do it unless you have to," I said. "It gives me the willies. I mean, jeez." I shuddered. And then, I felt my face beginning to bulge out.

"Rachel!"

"I'm cool. I'm cool," I said. I took a deep breath and let go of the grossed-out feeling I'd had about being morphed. The allergic morph stopped and my face returned to normal.

"Hey! You! The Falling Girl! Come on!"

The clipboard woman came rushing past and grabbed my arm, pulling me down the hall.

"Okay, listen up because we're desperately late. You go on in the last segment. I'll tell you when to go. You walk across the stage to Barry. He'll shake your hand. Then Cindy Sue will shake your hand, unless she's in a snit. Then you sit. Don't worry about which camera to look at, just look at Barry and Cindy Sue. Barry and Cindy Sue will ask you about all this alligator stuff —"

"Crocodile," I corrected.

"You tell them your little story. If Barry does *this* with his hand, that means speed up. If he does *this* with his hand, it means wrap it up because we're done. Got it? Good. Nothing to worry about."

She stopped suddenly and stared at Cassie. "Who are you?"

"I'm Falling Girl's partner, Dropping Chick," Cassie said.

Clipboard woman stared at her.

"She's my friend," I said. "You know, for moral support."

"Yeah, whatever. Come on. Our greenroom

can't be used. We had some band on the show last week and they trashed the place." She was still yanking me along by my arm, which would have made me mad. Except that I couldn't get mad. Or sad. Or anything, without setting off an allergic reaction.

Clipboard woman planted Cassie and me on two tall stools. We were in a dark corner, up against a cinder block wall covered in wires and cables and switches.

Bart Jacobs, the animal guy, was sitting on an identical stool. He was smoking a cigarette and talking to one of his animal handlers.

Lined up against the cinder block wall were half a dozen cages filled with Bart Jacobs's animals. A lion cub. A baby elephant. A python. A golden eagle.

From our gloomy corner we could see out onto the familiar *Barry and Cindy Sue* set. It was made up to look like a living room, with comfy-looking chairs clustered in the center. Facing the chairs were the cameras — one on each side and one right in the middle.

Beyond the brilliant light of the set was a studio audience. Not that I could see them. They were in darkness, and the lights on the set blinded me for anything else.

Then, in a rush, Barry himself came blowing

past. "Hello, everyone, we're looking for a great show today. Hope you're all really up. Up! Up! Energy! Keep that energy high! See you out there!"

Ten seconds later, Cindy Sue swept by in a wave of perfume, followed by a man who was trying to comb Cindy Sue's hair as she walked.

She flashed a fake smile at me and a disdainful look at Bart Jacobs.

The animal guy leaned close to me, took his cigarette out of his mouth and said, "She's never forgiven me for one of my little beasties wetting on her dress."

From out beyond the lights I heard the welcoming roar of the audience. I saw my dad standing on the far side of the set, talking to clipboard woman. He saw me and flashed a smile and a wink.

I was not nervous. I was not scared. No emotion. No emotion. It was the only way. I could do it. I *could*.

Barry and Cindy Sue were chatting out on stage. Then Jeremy Jason came blowing past like a small thunderstorm. He looked mad. I heard him mutter to a frightened-looking man, "What do you mean the greenroom is closed? You can't keep me standing around! I'm Jeremy Jason McCole!"

Of course, he was probably not really Jeremy Jason McCole anymore. *He was probably a Controller*, I reminded myself. Right now, the real Jeremy Jason was caged in a corner of his own mind. He was watching helplessly as the Yeerk controlled his every movement, his every action, his every word.

Was it beginning to occur to the vain, ambitious jerk that he had been tricked? Had he realized yet that there is no such thing as partnership with a Yeerk?

The Yeerk is master. The human host is a slave. Period. And when the infestation is voluntary, the human slave is even weaker. Even less able to resist.

It made me sick to think of it. Jeremy Jason had asked for it. He'd let himself be tricked. Still, it made me sick . . .

Wait a minute. I *did* feel sick.

Oh, no, I pleaded silently. *Not now.*

I looked at Cassie. "Cassie? I don't think I'm going to make it."

"What do you mean? Look, if you're scared or whatever, you just have to control the emotion."

I shook my head. "It's not that. I feel . . . weird. I feel distorted. I feel like something is happening inside me."

"The allergic morphing?"

"I don't think so. I have that under control for now. I think maybe I'm having that thing."

"What thing?"

"You know."

"The *hereth illint*? Now? Here? Now?"

I nodded. "Yeah. Here. Now."

CHAPTER 21

"Oh, no," Cassie wailed.

But she wailed quietly, because Bart Jacobs was still sitting next to us. He was talking to his assistants and getting ready to go out on stage.

Barry had finally finished telling a funny story. The audience roared with laughter. Cindy Sue was starting to introduce the animal guy. He stood up and straightened his clothes. An assistant came rushing up with a leash for Bart to take. On the end of it was the llama.

<Hi again,> Marco said. <Hey. We're in show biz! I always knew I'd make it. Maybe I didn't exactly expect to make it as a llama . . .>

". . . here he is, Bart Jacobs!"

Applause. Bart moved out, dragging Marco

126

along behind him. His assistants were already lining up the other animals. Jeremy Jason was in a dark corner having an angry conversation with someone.

Meanwhile, I was falling apart.

Ax hadn't mentioned that *hereth illint* is extremely unpleasant. It started with a wave of such intense nausea I almost launched my lunch right then and there. But behind the sick stomach came something much worse. Total disorientation. My body was rejecting the crocodile DNA. But the croc inside me didn't go peacefully. Before it could leave, it surfaced inside me. I could feel the cold, calculating crocodile mind bubbling up within my own.

I was losing control of my own body!

At exactly the same time, in the same body, two completely separate brains were looking out at the world through my eyes. The croc was nervous. He wasn't used to this. He didn't know where he was.

But crocodiles aren't just brainless, ruthless killing machines. They are *smart*, ruthless killing machines. And the crocodile got right past the fact that it was in a place no crocodile should ever be. It got right to the important stuff. It focused on what it needed to do.

And what it needed to do was eat.

The crocodile tried to swish its tail. But it didn't

have a tail. So it shook my . . . our . . . no, *my* butt.

"Rachel! What are you doing?"

"I . . . I'm not . . ," I managed to say. Then the crocodile decided he was tired of trying to swim. He was just going to run after his prey. And he did have legs.

Before I could even resist, I was racing across the floor, waving my arms like an idiot and shuffling like a demented lunatic. I raced right at Jeremy Jason McCole.

Right at him, with my massive crocodile jaws open for the quick kill!

Except that I didn't have crocodile jaws.

"Ahhhh!" Jeremy Jason yelled as I bit down on his shoulder.

Cassie grabbed me and yanked me off him. "She's a big fan, Jeremy Jason! She loves you!"

"Get this crazy girl away from me!" Jeremy Jason cried.

I tried to bite Cassie.

Bart Jacobs's assistant led Marco offstage and another shoved a giant tortoise out into the lights.

<I killed out there,> Marco said. <They love me — hey! Hey!>

I bit Marco on the neck. Fortunately, human teeth aren't very deadly.

Cassie dragged me off and now, a little too

late, I was beginning to be Rachel again. But that wasn't the end of my problems. Because even as my human mind rose to the surface again, I felt my weight increase. I felt unbelievably heavy. And I felt the back of my outfit stretch and strain. It tugged at my neck and sleeves.

Suddenly, I was the Hunchback of Notre Dame. Something very large was growing on my back. And I had a really bad feeling I knew what it was.

Now I understood what Ax had been talking about. See, I knew the crocodile DNA was going to be expelled from my system. I just didn't realize it would become a full-grown, twenty-foot-long killing machine in the process.

But what's sad is that even this wasn't the worst of it. See, the whole thing was making me very upset. I was mad. I was scared. I was mad at how scared I was. I was a whole basket of extreme emotion.

And I wasn't rid of my allergy just yet.

CHAPTER 22

"Rachel!" Cassie gasped.

"I know!" I said.

"We have to get out of here!"

"I know!"

Cassie grabbed me and quick-stepped me off the stage. We brushed rudely past Jeremy Jason, who recoiled in horror from the looney girl who'd bitten him.

We brushed past the clipboard woman who yelled, "Hey, stop! You can't leave!"

"She has to blow chunks!" Cassie said. "I think it's stage fright."

"Down the hall. On the left!"

By the time we reached the ladies' room, I was beyond hunchback. I looked like a buffalo.

"What are we going to do?" Cassie asked.

"Like I know?" I shrilled. "I have a crocodile coming out of my back! And . . . and I think I'm . . . grrr . . . rroowwwr!" I looked in horror at my hands. Yes, thick brown fur was growing. Fur I knew well.

Grizzly bear fur.

"Ax said you have to focus! Control the process! Or something like that."

I glared furiously at Cassie. I could no longer speak. I was making a warp speed change to grizzly bear. And not just the feet this time. My blunt muzzle was protruding. My fingers were growing short while my fingernails were becoming the black, hooked claws that could disembowel an elk.

And at the same time, the crocodile was emerging from my back. It was literally crawling and squirming out of me.

It didn't hurt. But oh, man, was it creepy. Creepy beyond any creepiness. And I'm a girl who's seen some creepy things.

"Oh, no!" Cassie whispered in utter horror, staring at whatever was happening on my back.

Someone tried to open the bathroom door.

"Go away! Occupied!"

"I have to go," a woman's voice whined.

"Trust me," Cassie grated. "Go somewhere else."

131

<Cassie!> I cried as soon as I got thought-speak. <This crocodile. He's not me. Do you understand? He's a real, out-of-control crocodile!>

Cassie shot a desperate glance around the bathroom. It was way too small to hold a twenty-foot crocodile as well as a grizzly bear.

<Cassie. The croc will kill you.>

Now the crocodile was so heavy it was weighing me down. And in the bathroom mirror I saw the horrendous image of a crocodile snout growing and emerging in the area just behind my own neck. I would have been knocked to the ground by the sheer weight of the reptile, but as he was growing, I was becoming the grizzly bear. And grizzly bears are extremely strong.

"I don't have a morph that can beat a crocodile!" Cassie said. "Nothing can fight a crocodile!"

<Then get out!>

"I can't! You're blocking the door with your crocodile tail!"

<Get in the stall! Quick! The head is almost formed!>

I saw myself reflected in the mirror. It was an image from the nightmares of a madwoman. It was insane! Two heads seemed to be growing from the same body: grizzly bear and crocodile. The croc snapped its toothy jaws, trying them out.

<Rachel, what if the crocodile attacks the bear?>

I was surprised to hear Cassie using thought-speak. <Cassie, are you morphing in there?>

<Yes!>

<To what?>

<Um . . . um . . . a squirrel!>

<A squirrel? A *squirrel*?!>

<It was all I could think of!>

I felt a slurping, sliding sensation. It was like my guts were being ripped out through my back, only it wasn't really painful. More like extremely nauseating.

Then I felt the weight drop off me. I heard a loud series of thuds.

The *hereth illint* was complete. I had "burped" the crocodile.

It lay splayed across the tile floor, its big tail wrapped uncomfortably in the corner, blocking the door.

As for me, I was fully grizzly bear now. I stood erect, with my big shaggy head brushing the acoustical tile ceiling. I felt the amazing power in my massive shoulders. I felt the invincibility of the grizzly bear.

Nothing that lived could take down a grizzly bear. Except . . . except for perhaps the huge reptile at my feet.

Over the top of the stall door I saw a squirrel,

hunkering down on the toilet seat, shaking and quaking in squirrel style.

<The crocodile is eyeing me,> I said. I felt terrible dread. You don't really know how deadly an animal is till you've *been* that animal.

I'd been the crocodile.

Grizzly bears are unbelievably powerful. They can swing their big paws and knock a horse to the ground. But the grizzly had no weapons to use on the crocodile. Not even the grizzly's ripping claws would tear a hole in the croc's scaly armor.

And once that crocodile latched its jaws onto any part of the bear, the bear . . . me . . . would be ripped apart, piece by piece.

The crocodile eyed me coldly. It smiled its toothy crocodile smile. And then it lunged.

CHAPTER 23

I saw a flash of teeth.

And then I saw a flash of gray.

A bushy tail and tiny hands and big brown eyes went rocketing past.

<Cassie!>

The gray squirrel leapt over the toilet stall door, flew through the air, landed on the crocodile's ancient dinosaur head and started scrabbling at its big slitted eyes.

The croc went nuts. It forgot about me, and began thrashing insanely in an attempt to throw off the squirrel.

And someone chose that very moment to try to get into the bathroom.

135

"I can't find another bathroom! I have to get in!" a woman said.

The crocodile thrashed its tail.

I lunged down at the crocodile, swiping with a paw the size of a canned ham.

And we all hit the bathroom door.

WHAM-BOOOM!

The door exploded from its hinges! Out rushed a crocodile with a squirrel on its head, and a grizzly bear.

"AHHHHHHH!" the woman screamed. I think she found another bathroom after that.

I tripped over the crocodile. I hit the floor. The croc was on me in a flash.

I tried to get up on all fours, but man, that crocodile was fast! With no time to get up, I could only power my way down the hall by clawing. I sunk six-inch claws into the walls and propelled myself, scooting along on my back, like some weird out-of-control grizzly skateboarder.

I scooted in terror, ripping the walls apart as I went. The croc scooted after me, snapping at the air just millimeters from my hind legs.

Cassie had almost been thrown. She was holding on to the croc's neck with all her strength, but she couldn't reach his eyes anymore.

And then, still scooting, I ran out of the hallway. With one last push I scooted on my back out into the backstage area, trailing a huge crocodile and a chittering, manic squirrel.

People standing around off the set began to notice us.

"Ahhhhhh!"

"Help! Help!"

"Run! Run! Ruuuuun!"

Suddenly, crocodile jaws caught my leg.

HhhhhoooRRRAAWWRRR! I bellowed in pain.

A llama broke free of a trainer's hand and rushed with insane courage at the crocodile. There was absolutely nothing Marco could do, but he tried anyway. And it didn't take a lot of time before he was thrown clear. But he scrambled right up, and came back for more.

"Get those animals out of here!" the clipboard woman screamed.

"They're not my animals! They're not my animals!" Bart Jacobs yammered as he ran to hide. "I don't know where they came from!"

The croc started thrashing, grinding the bones in my leg. It was literally trying to tear my leg off!

And it hurt.

It hurt a lot.

ROOOWWWWR!

"Oh, no! The show will be ruined!"

"Should we go to commercial?"

"Who cares? Run! Ahhhhh!"

CHAPTER 24

Maybe it was the sight of the brave-but-insane charge of the llama. Or maybe it was the fact that Cassie was once more scrabbling at the crocodile's eyes. But he opened his jaws just an inch.

Just enough.

I yanked my crushed leg out of the croc's mouth and tried to get far enough away that I could turn and fight head-on. Like that would work.

Unfortunately, this move ended up dragging the entire battle — grizzly bear, squirrel, llama, and crocodile — out onto the set.

Out to where Barry and Cindy Sue were gamely trying to interview Jeremy Jason McCole.

Out to where Jeremy Jason McCole was just starting to say, "Barry and Cindy Sue, I'm involved with this group that I think is really a wonderful organization. I think —"

Out to where brilliant lights illuminated our snarling, snapping, slashing, chittering, roaring ball of fur, claws, tails, scales, and teeth.

Barry leapt out of his chair and backed away at amazing speed.

Cindy Sue was cool. She just kept saying, "Can we get Bart Jacobs to come out here and remove his animals?"

Of course Bart knew better than to get involved in a fight between a crocodile and a bear. "They aren't my animals, you silly twit!" he yelled at Cindy Sue.

It was Jeremy Jason who was most surprising. He didn't run away. He didn't scream. He froze. He froze as stiff as a statue. The only thing that moved was his eyes. They kept growing larger.

That's when I noticed an Andalite had emerged, though he kept himself beyond the range of the cameras. And he carefully stayed there. It was Ax!

<What does it take to stop this thing?> Cassie asked me desperately, as she tried to rake over the croc's eyes.

<More than any of us has,> I said grimly.

Suddenly, the crocodile jerked its entire body

139

with incredible violence. I was in grizzly bear morph, and I never would have believed anything was that much stronger than a grizzly. But when the crocodile thrashed, we all knew it.

Cassie had been thrown. Much farther than Marco. I lost sight of her as she was flying through the air, squirrel tail flapping like the tail on a kite.

And now there was nothing between me and the crocodile.

This was an animal that fed by dragging full-grown wildebeests and impalas into the river. I was bigger than its normal meals. But this crocodile had a grudge against me. It had started to chow down and I'd gotten away. And it didn't like that.

It came for me. And let me tell you something: You do not ever, ever, *ever* want a crocodile looking at you for dinner.

Was I scared? Oh, yes. If I stood and fought, I'd lose. Period.

<Okay, that does it,> Jake said. <We are out of here!>

Jake. He'd caught up to us. And he didn't sound happy.

Then in my head I heard Cassie's thought-speak voice. <I'm at the light switches! I think I can turn off the lights! Get ready to run!>

<What?>

<When the lights go down, everyone bail!> Cassie cried.

<I'm ready,> Marco said.

And that's when fate intervened. Marco was climbing to his llama feet. His hooves splayed suddenly on the waxed floor and he plowed into the back of Jeremy Jason's seat.

The actor — or the Yeerk in his head — was still frozen in horror. And he stayed frozen as he fell from the chair and landed directly in front of the crocodile.

CHAPTER 25

The audience screamed in renewed horror.

Cindy Sue finally broke and ran.

Barry was yelling ridiculous directions in total panic. "Get a stapler! Get a stapler!"

I think that's what he was saying, anyway. I was a little distracted.

Jeremy Jason was no longer frozen. "Ahhhhh! Ahhhhh! Save me! Save me! Get it off me!"

And with my dim bear vision, I could have sworn I saw something slimy and gray come crawling out of Jeremy Jason's ear.

And that's when the lights went out.

<Okay, run for it!> Cassie cried.

Sudden darkness! Not pitch-black, but too dark for cameras or the audience to see.

Total pandemonium in the audience. It's one thing to see wild animals up on a set. It's a whole different feeling, sitting in the dark and not knowing whether those wild animals are going to come rampaging into the audience.

The entire studio was nothing but screams. Screams and animal roars. And above it all, the shrill, horrified scream of Jeremy Jason.

"Save me! Save me!"

I saw a rush of movement from offstage.

Suddenly an Andalite was leaping through the air. It landed directly on the crocodile's back. The Andalite tail flashed.

Flashed!

Flashed!

Flashed!

And suddenly the crocodile let go of Jeremy Jason.

<Ax?> I asked.

<Yes,> he said, sounding grim.

I knew Andalites are tougher than they look. I'd fought alongside Ax before. But nothing ever impressed me as much as that. That crocodile was a tank. It was unstoppable!

And now it was stopped.

<Where's the Yeerk?> I asked Ax.

<I saw the Yeerk leave this human a few seconds ago.>

So I *had* seen a slug crawling out of Jeremy

143

Jason! The Yeerk had panicked. It didn't want to be swallowed up along with its host body.

It was crawling around on the dark stage like a snail without its shell.

<Everyone okay?> Jake asked.

<Yeah,> I answered.

<Alive,> Marco said. <Not happy, but alive.>

<Then let's get out of here!> Jake yelled.

<Definitely,> I agreed fervently. I looked down at the stilled crocodile head. You know, even dead, it just scared the pee out of me.

Possibly because it was still very close to a yelling, screaming, cursing, hysterical Jeremy Jason McCole.

I bailed. I ran for the far side of the stage. But as I ran, I felt one of my massive bear paws step on something.

Something warm and squishy.

Something that felt like a slug.

<I don't think the Yeerk made it too far,> I said.

CHAPTER 26

We demorphed in the ladies' room. Ax did the opposite, morphing into his human form.

But we had lost Cassie.

"I'll find her," I said. "You guys get out of here. I'm supposed to be here. But we can't explain why you're here."

I headed back toward the set area. It was still dark. Whatever Cassie had done to the lights, it was taking a while to fix them.

There was an awful lot of shouting going on. A lot of unpleasant language was being used.

I turned a corner and practically plowed into the back of a man who was standing there. He didn't even turn around. He was staring intently at a person standing just in front of him.

I heard a voice say, "Yeah, can you believe my luck?"

The voice seemed strange and familiar at the same time. Like I had heard it before, but not quite this way.

Then I realized.

"I mean, I fall in a crocodile pit, my house falls down on me, and now this."

I raised up on tiptoes and looked over the man's shoulder. What I saw was me. Me.

Actually Cassie, morphed into me.

The man she was talking to was one of the show's producers.

"You're a very unlucky girl," the man said.

"That's what I keep telling people," Cassie said. "They keep saying how lucky I am to survive. I keep saying, like, *not*!"

He nodded. "You know, for a moment there I wondered about you . . . ," he said, letting the sentence trail off. Then he shrugged. "But the crocodile has been destroyed. And yet here you are."

I flattened myself back against the wall. If he turned and saw me he'd definitely flip. And what if he was a Controller? I couldn't take that chance.

"Yeah, I'm glad it didn't get me," Cassie said. "I'm getting out of here. I have to find my dad.

He's here somewhere. It would help if someone would like, you know, get things organized."

Cassie pushed past the man. I turned my face away, not wanting to surprise her.

"Andalite!" the man snapped.

My heart stopped. He was testing Cassie. Waiting to see if she would react. If she would recognize the word. If Cassie hesitated or stopped he would know.

He would know.

I shouldn't even have worried.

When he rapped out the word "Andalite!" she kept walking and without hesitation said, "Yeah, a light would be helpful, too."

The man made a snorting, dismissive sound and turned away.

I fell into step behind Cassie. "Nice job, sister," I said.

"Oh, good, you're back," she said. "It's a good thing. I'm having the worst time trying to control this morph!"

"You're having trouble being me? What could be hard about that?"

She raised an eyebrow in a way that looked as much like Cassie as it did like me. "This brain of yours. It keeps trying to get me to do really dumb things."

Paramedics came rushing past us, shoving us

apart. When we were alone again I said, "Hey, I said we were going to improvise, right? And look how well it all turned out. We're all alive. Jeremy Jason probably won't be endorsing anything for a while, let alone The Sharing. Plus, I stepped on the Yeerk."

"Jake will still kill you."

I laughed. "Cassie, if I were Jake, I'd kill me, too. Say . . . I don't suppose you'd want to stay in my body a while longer . . ."

"Nope."

"Coward."

"Yep."

CHAPTER 27

Two days later, we sat around watching TV up in my hotel room. It would be another week at least till my house was rebuilt.

In the meantime, there was room service. And cable TV.

We lounged around, eating pie. The Animorphs. Cassie, the ecology nut, animal girl; Marco, who thought everything was a joke; and our fearless yet modest leader, Jake.

There was also a disturbingly pretty boy named Ax — a boy who was actually an Andalite when he wasn't in human morph. Ax's entire face was covered with pie. Ax doesn't have a mouth in his normal body, and the sense of taste totally overwhelms him when he morphs human. The boy is dangerous around food.

And standing on the windowsill there was a fierce red-tailed hawk. Tobias didn't want pie.

We watched TV and picked at remnants of pie crust as familiar theme music started to play.

Marco invented his own lyrics and sang along. "*Entertainment Tonight*, we're so glib and so light. *Entertainment Tonight*, we got stars all right! We'll entertain you and drain you of all your thoughts tonight, yeah, yeah, yeah yeah!"

Jake threw a pillow and hit Marco in the back of his head.

"Shh," Cassie said. "Here it comes."

The male announcer said, "You'll all remember the story we reported yesterday of the incredible melee during the broadcasting of the *Barry and Cindy Sue Show*. Wild animals brought to the show by Bart Jacobs broke loose and created a terrible scene, during which Jeremy Jason McCole, the young star of the hit television series *Power House*, was nearly eaten by a crocodile.

"Well, today we have an update. Jeremy Jason McCole is out of the hospital. Doctors say he'll be fine. But in an amazing development, his agent says Jeremy Jason is quitting *Power House* and leaving the country. McCole's agent refuses to divulge the young actor's whereabouts, but sources say he has been spotted in Uzbekistan, a small central Asian nation."

<Uzbekistan?> Tobias repeated.

"I guess that was as far as he could get from the Yeerks and the media," I suggested.

"I wonder if they have crocodiles in Uzbekistan?" Marco wondered.

"I'm guessing no," I said. "I don't think Jeremy Jason McCole will ever get within a thousand miles of a crocodile again."

"Or a Yeerk. At least if he can help it," Jake said.

Cassie sighed loudly.

"What is it, Cassie?" Jake asked.

She sighed again. "It's just a pity. He really was cute."

"Mmmm," I agreed. "Those dimples."

"That hair."

"Those eyes."

"Those lips."

"Ax," Marco said. "You should have let the crocodile eat him."

I ignored Marco, as I usually do. "He was, without a doubt, the cutest guy ever."

"That does it," Jake said. "Marco? Change the channel. Put on *Baywatch*."

I reached over and tried to snatch the remote away from Marco, but he was too quick. He flipped through the channels and then said, "Ah, there we go."

I looked up, expecting to see red bathing suits. Instead, I saw swords and leather boots.

Xena: Warrior Princess. My kind of girl.

Marco winked at me.

"Well, okay," I said. "*This* we can watch."

<Hork-Bajir!> Rachel snarled.

A year ago that name would have meant nothing to me. It would have just been some nonsense word.

But now I knew the Hork-Bajir. The Andalite who gave us our powers had told us the Hork-Bajir were once a decent, peaceful species. But they had been enslaved by the Yeerks. All of them were Controllers now. The entire species carried the Yeerk slugs in their heads.

And with the Yeerks controlling their every action, the Hork-Bajir were walking killing machines.

Amazingly fast. Incredibly strong. Armored,

bladed, almost fearless. They were the shock troops of the Yeerk empire.

Hork-Bajir had come close to killing Rachel several times. And all of us had felt the Hork-Bajir blades at least once.

<What is a Hork-Bajir doing, coming out in broad daylight?> Rachel asked.

I looked closely. The Hork-Bajir was climbing some kind of ladder. When it reached the surface, it blinked its reptilelike eyes at the light. It climbed out and stood like some vision of a demon. Then I noticed that there was a second Hork-Bajir coming up behind it.

<There are two of them!> Rachel said.

<Yeah. And you know what? I think they look scared.>

Just then . . .

SKREEEET! SKREEEET! SKREEEET!

The alarm horn was deafening to my hawk hearing. The sound screamed up from the hole in the ground. The two Hork-Bajir jerked in surprise and fear. One of them grabbed the other and held it close for a split second. In an instant, they were off and running through the forest.

Running as if their lives depended on it.

And let me tell you something — Hork-Bajir can move out when they want. Those big, long legs take big, long steps. They plowed into the brush, slashing wildly with their bladed arms, slicing through bushes and thorns and small trees like a harvester going through a wheat field.

<How are you doing on morph time?> I asked Rachel.

<I still have an hour at least,> she said.

<So we follow these guys?>

<Oh, yeah.>

We flapped to gain some of the altitude we'd lost and prepared to follow the Hork-Bajir. Not much of a challenge, really. They were chopping a path straight through the woods that a blind man could follow.

<They're not exactly into the stealth thing, are they?> Rachel commented.

And that's when things really broke loose. Up from the hole in the ground humans poured. Armed humans. Men and women, dressed in an array of normal-looking human clothing.

Controllers, of course. Not that you could tell by looking. But I knew now that that hole led down to the Yeerk pool. And there was no doubt in my mind — these humans were human-Controllers. Slaves to the Yeerks in their heads.

They carried human weapons — automatic rifles, handguns, shotguns.

The Yeerks were going after the two Hork-Bajir. But they were being careful. They were sending only human-Controllers. They weren't going to risk any more Hork-Bajir being seen by normal people.

Twenty . . . thirty human-Controllers climbed up out of the hole.

<They'll never catch them,> Rachel said.

<I know. What is going on here? Are those Hork-Bajir trying to escape somehow?>

Up from the hole machines began to appear. They seemed to levitate. I almost laughed when I saw them.

<Dirt bikes? The Yeerks have motorcycles?> It seemed bizarre, even funny. The Yeerks have faster-than-light spacecrafts. Now they were using dirt bikes?

<Uh-oh,> Rachel said. <The Hork-Bajir are fast, but they aren't *that* fast.>

VrrrrRRRROOOM! VrrrrRRRROOOM! Vrrrr-RRRROOOOM!

Human-Controllers were firing up the motorcycles. I could hear the sputtering roar of the engines. In all, fifteen Yamahas and Kawasakis came up through that hole.

VrrrrRRRROOOM! Vrrrrraaaa-vrrrraaa-vraaaa!

The motorcycles took off. Some had just one rider. Others had two — one to steer and one to shoot.

The Hork-Bajir had a lead of a few hundred yards, but they'd never outrun this small army.

As I watched from the safety of the air above, the motorcycles roared off through the woods in pursuit. They churned up dirt and leaves and shattered the quiet.

And they gained quickly on the two fleeing Hork-Bajir.

Blam! Blam! Blam! Blam!

Rifles barked. Motorcycles roared! The Hork-Bajir ran, but the bikes leapt and twisted and snaked toward them.

Blam! Blam! Blam!

Bambambambambambambambam!

Rifles, automatic weapons, and shotguns all ripped apart the tree trunks. The human-Controllers were firing wildly. Firing at anything that moved. From the ground they couldn't see the Hork-Bajir yet. But they could see flashes of them, and they kept on shooting.

<This is going to be all over in about ten seconds,> Rachel said grimly. <What are we going to do?>

<You want to help Hork-Bajir?> I asked incredulously.

<Have you ever heard the saying, "the enemy of my enemy is my friend"? The Yeerks want these two Hork-Bajir dead. That's good enough for me.>

<Me, too,> I said. <We'll have to use thought-speak. Talk directly to them.>

<Let's do it,> Rachel said.

I would have smiled if I'd had a mouth. Rachel is so brave she's just short of being reckless.

I like that about her.

<Hey. Hork-Bajir down there.>

I saw them stagger, as though they were shocked and amazed to be hearing thought-speak. Like *that* was their major problem.

<You're about ten seconds away from being dead,> I said. <Listen to me and you just might get out of this alive.>

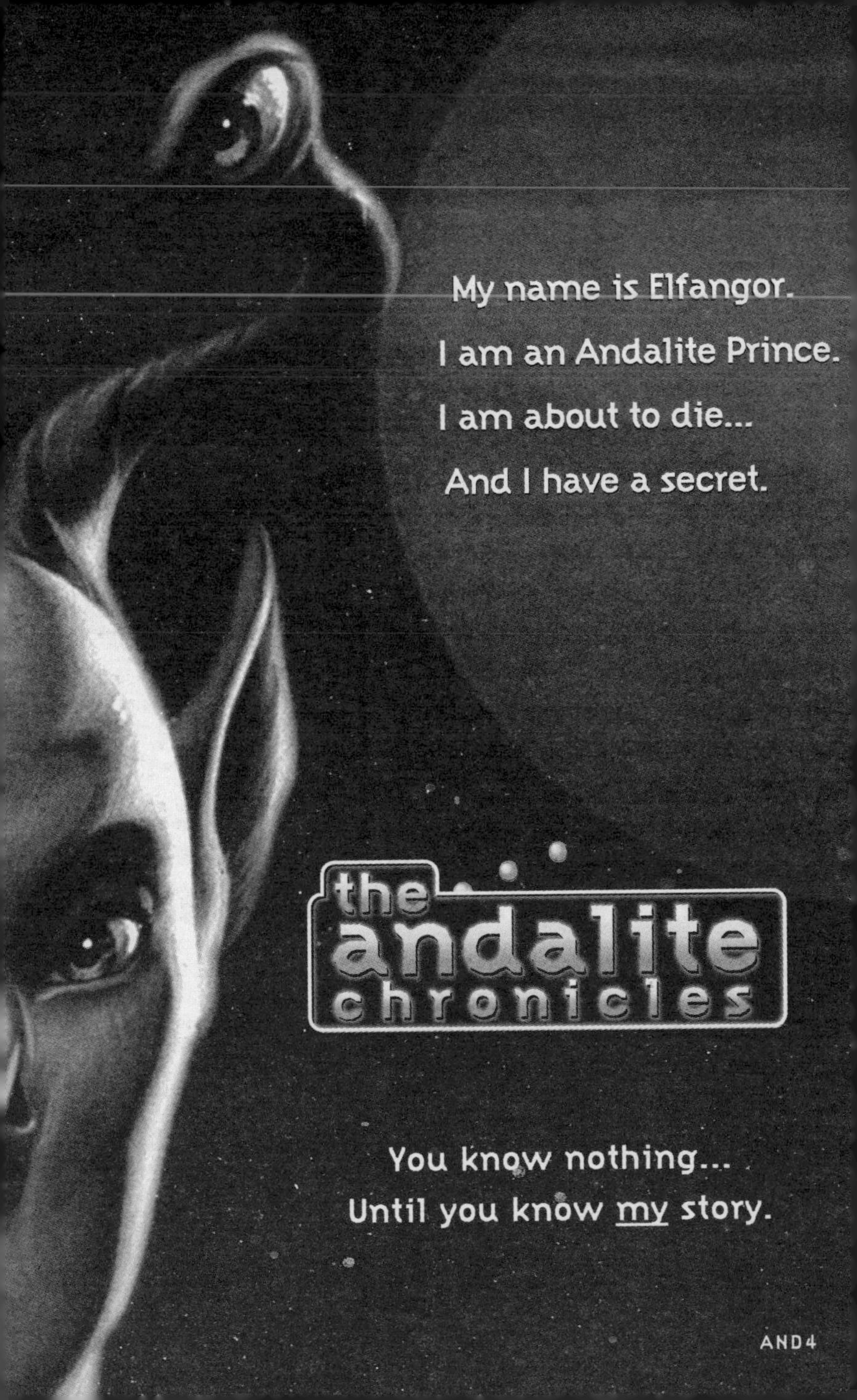
My name is Elfangor.
I am an Andalite Prince.
I am about to die...
And I have a secret.
the andalite chronicles
You know nothing...
Until you know my story.
AND4

My name is Elfangor.

I am an Andalite prince. And I am about to die.

My fighter is damaged. I have crash-landed on the surface of the planet called Earth. I believe that my great Dome ship has been destroyed. I fear that my little brother Aximili is already dead.

We did not expect the Yeerks to be here in such force. We made a mistake. We underestimated the Yeerks. Not for the first time. We would have defeated their Pool ship and its fighters. But there was a Blade ship in orbit as well.

The Blade ship of Visser Three.

Two Yeerk Bug fighters are landing on either side of me now. The abomination Visser Three is here as well. I can feel him. I can sense his evil.

I cannot defeat the visser in one-on-one combat. I am weak from my injuries. Too weak to morph. Too weak to fight.

This is my *hirac delest* — my final statement.

I have formed the mental link to the thought-speak transponder in my fighter's computer. I will record my memories before the Yeerks annihilate all trace of me.

If this message someday reaches the Andalite world, I want the truth to be known. I am called a great warrior. A hero. But there is a great deal that no Andalite knows about me. I have not lied, but I have kept the truth a secret.

This is not my first visit to Earth. I spent many years on Earth . . . and yet, no time at all.

I landed here now in this construction site because I was looking for a great weapon: the Time Matrix. The existence of this weapon is also a secret.

So many secrets in my life . . . mistakes. Things I should have done. All the strands of my strange life seem to be coming together. It all seems inevitable now. Of course my death would come on Earth. Of course the child would be here. Of course it would be Visser Three who would take my life.

I am too weak to locate the Time ship now. I will die here. But I have left a legacy. Visser Three thinks he has won our long, private war. But I've left a little surprise behind.

I have given the morphing power to five human youths.

I know that in doing this I have broken Andalite law. I know that this action will be condemned by all my people. But the Yeerks are here on Earth. Visser Three is here. The humans must be given a chance to resist. The human race cannot fall to the Yeerks the way the Hork-Bajir race did.

I have given the morphing power to five young humans. Children, really. But sometimes children can accomplish amazing things.

I have no choice but to hope. Because it was I who created Visser Three. I who caused the abomination. I cannot go peacefully to my death, knowing that I created the creature who will enslave the human race.

I came to this place, this empty construction site, looking for the weapon I know is hidden here. But there is no time now. No time . . .

The visser is here. He is laughing at my weakness. He is savoring his victory over me.

This is the *hirac delest* of Elfangor-Sirinial-Shamtul, Andalite prince. I open my mind in the ritual of death. I open my mind and let all my memories — all my secrets — go to be recorded by the computer.

This is not just a message to my own people. I hope that someday humans will read it as well. Because humans are also my people. Loren . . . and the boy I have just met, but not for the first time. . . .

Sometimes there's no turning back.

Or maybe there is.

I felt myself floating. Hanging in the air, only there wasn't any air. I wasn't flying, just floating.

There was light, a beautiful blue-green sort of light. It didn't come from any one place, though. It just seemed to be coming from everywhere at once.

One thing was for sure—I was not in the forest anymore.

HELLO, TOBIAS. WE MEET AGAIN.

The voice was huge, but not harsh. It filled my brain and seemed to resonate throughout my body. My feathers quivered. My fingers tingled.

Fingers?

And only then did I realize that I was changed.

ANIMORPHS #13: THE CHANGE

COMING IN NOVEMBER

K.A. Applegate

morphs is a trademark of Scholastic Inc. Copyright © 1997 by K.A. Applegate. All rights reseved. Printed in the U.S.A.   ANIT497

You Got Morphed!

What animal would you most want to morph into and why?

"A jaguar! It's fast, slim, angelic, sleek, calm under danger, fierce, and free."

Andre H., Age 12
Winner #3 of the Get Morphed contest

ANIMORPHS™

K.A